# A
# JOLLY
# GOOD
# FELLOW

# A
# JOLLY
# GOOD
# FELLOW

by
Stephen V. Masse

## REVIEW COPY

Good Harbor Press • Boston

*A Jolly Good Fellow*
Copyright © 2008 Stephen V. Masse
Good Harbor Press • Boston

For further information, please contact:
svm@goodharborpress.com

Book design by:
Arbor Books, Inc.
19 Spear Road, Suite 301
Ramsey, NJ 07446
www.arborbooks.com

Printed in the United States of America

*A Jolly Good Fellow*
Stephen V. Masse
1. Title  2. Author  3. Fiction

Library of Congress Control Number:  2007906833

ISBN 10:  0-9799638-0-X
ISBN 13:  978-0-9799638-0-3

Dedicated to the fond memory of
Henry A. Christopher
and
Nora Baldassarre Mustone

The small man builds cages
for everyone he knows.
While the sage,
who has to duck his head when the moon is low,
keeps dropping keys all night long
for the beautiful rowdy prisoners.
—Hafiz

I am indeed grateful to the many people who have given me support and inspiration in writing this book, especially my parents and family. The Coffee Shop crowd in Amherst was a vibrant source of peer review and friendship, and I thank Jay Neugeboren, Bret Lott, Stephen B. Oates, Alden Miller, Matt Snow, Phil Szczepanski, Kristin Shippey, Kyle Hoffman, Lyn Brennan Blake and Tina Gerakaris. Ron MacGillvray Jr. provided the use of his early Apple Macintosh before I was able to afford my first computer. Amanda VanTreese encouraged me through two re-writes, and John Michael Williams provided editorial coaching that saved the day. Thanks also to Riva Poor and Mark Spencer for their fine editorial skills, and Steven DeRosa for his eagle eyes. A special thanks to Carla Anne Vasta and Cosette Hirschfeld for their heartfelt applause, Carole Montone and family, Anthony Romano and family, Erik Viggh and family, Father Frank Jay, Henry F. Scannell, Kevin Flanagan, Jacqueline Dunn, Mida VanZuylen Dunn, Ron and Sharon Chait, Tony Pelusi Jr., and Michael Kent.

# REVIEW COPY

# TAPE ONE

He's out there hitchhiking. I'm driving back up West Border Parkway in the morning snow, and I know right off it's him because I watched him come out of his house three times last month, and just saw him go in the variety store all alone about twenty minutes ago, hanging around while the school bus came and then took off without him.

He looks in the car window quickly, then opens the door and piles right in. He rubs his hands together and breathes on them. I can see they're pretty red from the cold. He's smaller than I thought he might be, like I could push or pull him with one hand. I look at his face, all rosy with a few snowflakes melting, though his eyes look unhappy or mad or something. "You okay over there?" I ask. "What's with the hitchhikin'— you forget somethin' at home?"

"Me? No. Just trying to get a ride."

"Where to? You skippin' school and goin' to the mall?"

He says nothing, just wipes his face with his hand.

"You really shouldn't be out there hitchhikin'."

1

He shrugs. Then he puts his fingers right in the defroster vents and shifts his feet, kicking the roll of duct tape on the floor. "Maybe I should just get out and try another ride." He puts his hand to where the door lever should be, but finds the stem part broken off.

"Let's not get hasty here," I says. "You're in outa the snow, you got nice warm heat. It's just not every day some kid jumps in my car. How's those hands? Warmer, I bet."

He looks at his hands. I can see they picked up some dust from the dashboard. He wipes them on his coat front, and it makes a kind of whistling sound. "This is a pretty old car," he says. "I never knew anybody that drove such an old car." Kid starts telling me his father has a brand new Jaguar XKR convertible that makes my car look like some dog butt jalopy.

"You're gettin' a little harsh there, don't you think? This car's a classic—a Dodge Dart with slant six engine. I'll betcha there's only five or six people that have one of these. How many hundreds have a Jag? Besides, you shouldn't be talking like that."

"Like what?"

"When I was a kid, I never said that kind of stuff in front of respectable adults. Think you'd have a careful mouth, coming from such a high class town as you do."

I can see he's a little scared. He keeps looking at me like he thinks I'm going to hurt him or something. Maybe he can see I'm scared too, with him suddenly here before my eyes.

Pretty soon we come up to a red light, and before I know it, he's fiddling with the broken door handle. I jam the brakes hard. "Whatta you think you're doin'?" I says.

"I—I was just trying to close the door tighter."

"Can't you see it's busted?" I says. "Don't you try that stuff, or else you'll get hurt. You get that?"

"What's everybody's problem with me today?" he says. "If you don't mind, your stinking door's loose and I don't feel like falling out."

Just as the light turns green, I catch a look at his face and see some tears. Now I feel kinda bad. "You don't need to cry," I says. "Just don't be messin' with the door, you won't get yourself in trouble."

"Easy for you to say. I'm already in trouble."

"For what?"

"Well for your information, primarily, blowing off school. Then, in case you didn't notice me out there hitchhiking? My mother'll kill me, and my father will ground me until I'm twenty-one. And plus, I'm stuck in this old car with you, and no airbags, and I don't think I should be doing this."

"Just don't worry," I says. But I realize I'm the guy with the worries. I figured and calculated a dozen different possible things, but never imagined him just jumping in my car.

We drive a while more and get into downtown by and by. He gets busy looking at the holiday decorations all around the city, and seems to calm down. "Now," I says, "you're in my car and not in your old man's hotshot convertible, which if you think about it, ain't too practical on a snowy day. And besides, if you love his car so much, how come you were so quick to take a ride with a stranger?"

"Can we just drive?"

"We are driving."

"If you really want to know, I was cold. And besides, nobody stops to pick up a kid."

"Except maybe a school bus?"

"Duhh—does it look like I want to be in school?"

"Don't look much like you want to be anywhere. Not school, not home, not in my stinking rattletrap jalopy, and I'm beginnin' to wonder how I got so lucky to get you, the Booker kid, all to myself?"

His eyes jump right to me. "Hey! What the—how do you know who I am? Do you work for my father?"

"I just know your name's Booker," I says.

"Do you work at my school?"

"Hardly, kid. So what's your first name?"

He don't answer me, just wrinkles up his forehead and shifts in his seat.

"Ain't you got a name, kid?"

He's irritated now, like he's more mad I'm trying to pry out his name than he is about getting driven off by a stranger. "Okay, it's Gabriel," he says almost too soft to hear.

I reach out my hand for a handshake, and he looks at it like he don't know what to do, so I wiggle my fingers until he finally puts his hand in mine and I shake it. "Nice to meet you," I says.

We drive a half block more and nobody talks. Then suddenly he says, "Pretty hammy name, isn't it? That's my mother's idea. Gabriel—sounds gimpy."

"How old are you, anyhow?"

"Eleven," he says, then he looks out the window again.

"Just like I thought," I says.

*   *   *

Back to my part of town, and I get the creepy feeling I shouldn't smuggle the kid in the apartment yet. All I can think of is if anybody sees me with some school kid, and school not out yet—maybe I should wait till dark. But I don't want to keep him out in broad daylight, snow or no snow. By luck there's only one guy out on the street when I drive down, and he's way up ahead getting in his car to drive away. I just park and get out, then go to the kid's side and let him out. "Follow me."

The kid does just what I say, so I don't have to get rough. He looks up and down the street at all the different apartment buildings standing shoulder to shoulder. It's a small street off of the main drag, has only a couple real old trees that the city keeps chopping branches from. Mostly professional people live here, so there's hardly anybody around during work hours. My building is a brick walk-up—four old granite steps and a big front door, and four floors. I'm on the third floor. We get inside with no problem except some snow to brush off of ourselves. This could be some easy money for me, I think. The kid seems quiet enough, maybe from being scared, but I'm keeping a close eye on him just in case. Inside, he starts gawking all around. He goes over to the stove and picks up the coffee pot. "Wow, my grandmother has one of these in the garden. She grows parsley from it." Then he sees the statue of Saint Joseph on the counter, picks it up.

"You gotta touch stuff?" I ask, taking the statue from him and looking it over. "This was broken once, I had to glue it back together."

He pulls his hands down to his sides, like he's ashamed.

"Oh, the hell," I says. "It don't matter. You're gonna be here a while, you might as well get used to it."

"You don't mind if I stay?"

I look at him, try to figure out if he means it for real. Maybe he thinks I'm a relative, or one of his father's flunkies. "Of course you're gonna stay."

"Because I need certain things," he says. "Like for breakfast, Cap'n Crunch and Fruit Loops, and Frosted Flakes. And Hostess Doughnuts. Then for lunch, macaroni and cheese, frozen pizza, stuff like that."

"Okay, okay. But I got work to do."

"Well then, just give me some money and I can go get some stuff myself."

"Wait just a minute here, kid. Number one, you don't go get nothin'. You stay right here."

"So what's so tough about me going to get some things? I'm old enough to buy lousy groceries."

"Because, smart guy. Ain't you got the idea of what this is all about?"

He looks at me again with them eyes. Then his lip starts to go like he's ready to say something a few times, but then he just keeps staring at me instead, and says nothing.

"Look, kid—we need to talk. Why do you think I brought you here?"

"Okay, so I'm not sure. Unless you're going to try to get gay with me or—"

"Whoa there, boy," I clap my hand over his mouth. "Let's not get complicated. Must be some nice pals you got, teaching you all that rotten stuff."

"Okay then, so what do you have me here for?"

I go in my room and take out the clothes line rope I saved under my bed. "Now you got the idea, kid?"

He shrugs his shoulders.

"This is for tying up your victim. I just kidnapped you."

He stops cold and looks right at me. "But—kidnapped me? I don't want to be kidnapped." He backs away, and I see his face turning pale and his eyes growing wider. I step closer to him, and he puts his arms out like he's trying to hold me away from him.

"Well, ain't that too bad. 'Cause number one, you're not just some runaway kid. I know who you are, and I know where you live. Number two, I know your old man is Winthrop Lowell Booker the Third, known to his loyal backstabbers in the State House as Win Booker. So just because I didn't have to grab you offa the street and duct tape your mouth shut and shove you in my trunk, don't mean I didn't kidnap you."

Now he looks at me more scared than I ever thought he could be. His breath is fast and ragged, and he shrinks back till his leg hits a chair. "But—" he puts his hand up to his neck. "You want to chop off my head and show it on the Internet?"

"Hey, hey—you're gettin' ahead of yourself here, kid." I put the rope down on the counter. "Nobody's choppin' anything. What do you think this is, Baghdad?"

"Who are you, anyway? What kind of money do you think you can get from my father?"

"Shhh. Calm down, kid, willya?"

"He won't pay anything."

"Oh, yeah? I betcha I can get a hundred thousand bucks to return you safe to home."

"No way, that's bull sh—"

I crack him on his hand, not very hard. "Watch the mouth!"

"I didn't mean it," he yelps, yanking his hand away to rub it. Boy, is this kid a case. He don't even get up and start swinging and throwing stuff around, like I'd do if I was a kid and somebody kidnapped me.

"But I ran away from home in the summer, and they didn't even come to look for me," he says.

"That's a lie if I ever heard one," I says.

"I did run away."

"They looked for you, and they worried, too."

"They sent my uncle to look—and the police."

"Same thing, ain't it?"

"I stayed away four days, and I found my own way home. When I got there they were sore," he says, and looks at me with them eyes again.

"What made you run away?"

"Nothing much. I just wanted a vacation. I took two hundred dollars and went for a bus ride to New Hampshire and bought a sleeping bag and some food. I went to live in the woods the whole time. Then I got tired of it, and took a bus home."

"Took two hundred bucks? That's a lot of money for a kid to steal."

"I didn't steal it," he says, like I'm supposed to know all the time.

"So how did you get it?"

"My own money. I save up my allowance."

"Allowance?"

"Yeah. I get fifteen dollars every week."

"And your father can't pay that hundred grand?"

He looks at me again, like he's studying me. "Well, I suppose he can. Not that he will, but I guess he can if he really wants to."

"So, there you go. You bet your life he'll pay." I go to the fridge and take out some milk. "Now—before we do anything else, we gotta get something to eat. You hungry?"

He looks around and shrugs his shoulders. "This kitchen is kind of crappy," he says.

"Hey—one more like that you're gonna get a cauliflower ear," I says, wagging my finger at him. "Sit down on that chair."

"That one? It's all shaky. And look at this, it's all dirty. My mother'll kill me if I get all that sh—stuff on my trousers."

"Trousers? Can't you call them pants?"

"Pants means underwear in England."

"Well, this ain't merry old England. And don't worry about your mom, kid. You ain't about to see her for a few days, anyhow."

"So, big deal. I didn't want to be home today, anyway." He goes to the sink and grabs an old sponge next to it, wets it up and starts washing the chair.

We eat some peanut butter and jelly sandwiches for lunch. He likes the way I make them, only he makes me cut the crust off of the bread. He eats two, and says I don't seem like much of a kidnapper because I use the best jelly, Smucker's grape, instead of making him eat just bread and water.

"Never mind—I'll show you kidnapper," I says. "The only reason you're gettin' this is because you ain't a troublemaker, see? And if you do make trouble, you'll be eatin' stale bread crusts and suckin' canal water."

"But if I don't make trouble, how come you want to tie me up with rope?"

"'Cause that's part of being kidnapped. Now just sit down so I can tie you up." I hear what I'm saying and I realize it's way off what I planned a dozen times, to just grab the kid and stuff a hand towel in his mouth, and wrap duct tape or rope around and around him while he fights and squirms and kicks.

"How come?" he asks. "For a long time?"

Some kid, a real character. "Well, as long as it takes for cripes sake," I says. "Don't worry, it ain't gonna hurt. Not unless you get wise, you hear?"

"Yeah, but it's going to get awfully boring." Then he waits a while and keeps still—just looks at me. Kind of a nice face to look at, he's missing a tooth at the side and it makes his words slip out kind of lispy when you least expect it. "Well," he says, "if you have to tie me up, can you do it in front of the television?" Television he calls it, not TV.

"Okay, okay," I says. He could have been worse, kicking and biting like in the shows. I look at him, still worried in a way. Maybe he's planning something wise. He seems a lot smarter than I thought a kid would be. He's giving me the willies, though. Just kinda keeps looking at me with them big brown eyes, scared a little and yet not so scared. "Well," I says finally, "what the hellya lookin' at?"

He looks down at the floor real quick. Then he don't look at me anymore.

\* \* \*

It takes ten minutes to get him tied up in front of the TV, he's so bossy about how I do it. "Not around the stomach too much, don't go near my neck, don't make it too tight around the wrists or else the hands go numb," on and on. And all the time he's asking how long he'll have to stay like that, and I says as long as it takes for me to get back from my work. He asks what I do for a job, and I says, "Charity work," kind of sarcastic, but he don't take it that way.

Finally, I'm free to go out and work my charity corner. It's a pretty good cash thing, this is my third year doing it. I have a real fancy Santa Claus outfit, the kind with a wig that covers your whole head, none of that cheapie Santa stuff that shows all your whiskers and hair through it. With that outfit and a beggar pot on the street and ringing my bell, not even a world-class detective would know the difference between me and the real Santa Claus. I never once got asked to show my I. D. card, which I have a fake one of anyhow. Out on the street is a good way to get that old Christmas feeling. "Money for the needy," I says, ring the bell like crazy, make eighty or a hundred bucks a day. And I'm the needy, I get the money.

I can see a lot going on today. There's people selling neck-ties, sweaters, jewelry, all kinds of things. Across the way a few people stop to play some Christmas tunes with horns. Later on the artist girl stops by. She comes around sometimes, sets up her stuff and draws sketches of people. She's pretty in a funky kind of way, sorta puts her face close when she talks. She drops a dollar in my beggar pot. "Someday I'm going to draw you," she says.

I nod, but I'm not paying much attention. I guess I'm still a little numb inside, like I can't quite believe I kidnapped Gabriel. I don't know about kid stuff, and I sure don't want to be hanging around at home. He'll probably be less scared if he knows I got stuff to do. It's kinda strange the way he let me tie him up, almost like he thought it was some kind of game or adventure.

What happens next while I'm ringing my bell, some guy looks familiar stops right in front of my beggar pot. He's staring at me and starts screwing up his face. He says, "I know you—Wagner! Duncan Wagner! I never knew you to play Santa Claus."

I couldn't believe my ears, and my eyes weren't telling me as much as I wanted to know. He tells me, "I can tell it's you by your laugh and your eyes."

"Well, damn. You look familiar," I says, getting fidgety.

"Don't you remember me, Dick Murphy?"

"Oh man—for cripes sake! From the Towne Diner! Richard F. X. Murphy. Last time I seen you was about ten, twelve years ago. What brings you to Boston, anyhow?"

"A job," he says, "and a woman, too." He pats my arm and says he has to get going.

"Well, wait. Do you work around here?"

"Sure, I'll see you again. We'll talk," he says, and pretty soon he disappears among the people.

If it wasn't old Dick Murphy. I remember that Towne Diner well, and I give out this real big laugh to think of the crazy fun we used to have there—old Nellie teaching me how to cook eggs, and Dick in the background telling me not to scramble them with a hammer like the Three Stooges. I remember the Daily Special signs Dick used to draw on the chalk board, like Hot Puppies and Beans with the hot dogs drawn on a leash. And the fortieth birthday party we had for Alice the boss, when somebody gave her a bra made from two cabbage leaves, and she wore it over her blouse half the night while everybody laughed till they almost fell over. That ho-ho-ho gets me a lot more dimes and quarters, mostly from kids. They like standing around and listening to a real laugh from a pretty classy looking Santa Claus. Funny, I ain't the least bit fat, but the kids don't care. Guess they know times are tough.

\*     \*     \*

I get to my door almost forgetting I'm in my Santa Claus suit. It was hard enough to wrestle it on in the first place, because I had to dress in the dark cellar without a mirror for the makeup. But I know there's no way I can let the kid see me dressed like this. It would give him another handle on me that could get me turned in. I lean my ear close to the door and I can hear the TV still on. I hurry back down the stairs all the way to the cellar and take off the costume as quick as I can, roll it up under my arm. I go back up the stairs, wiping the red cheeks and cherry nose with a rumpled tissue.

Real easy, I open the door and sneak in. I look in the den, and what do I see? No kid. He's gone—out of the chair with the ropes left right there. Now I'm so mad I can't see straight. I nearly have myself a heart attack, run in my room and look out the front window to see if the kid is just on his way down the three stories of fire escape. No kid.

I drop my Santa Claus suit on the floor. Then I turn around and suddenly see the kid lying curled up on my bed sound asleep, with his hand all mushed up under his cheek.

# TAPE TWO

I'm almost ready to wake the kid up, but then I look down at the Santa suit. I hurry up and put it away and pull the cash bag out of my pants. I toss the money in the dresser drawer by my bed where I keep all my money, then go in the bathroom to wash off the rest of my makeup. I make sure to flush the red tissue down the toilet.

All the time I'm wondering why the hell this kid is still in my house. I wake him up. "Hey, hey. How come you untied the ropes, there, kid?" I ask. He turns over and looks at me, then jumps back a little.

"Huhn? I had to go to the bathroom," he says, all of a sudden scared.

"Then what the hell?—I don't understand you, kid."

"I was tired. I wanted a rest."

"Yeah," I says. I look at him and shake my head. Then I look at my old watch. "Hey, it's gettin' late. You hungry again?"

He sits up on the bed and looks at me. "I dunno," he says. He's got lines on his face, and his hair's got this shelf design from the pillow. He don't look too friendly. "Maybe I am and maybe I'm not. I can't tell after I just wake up."

I reach over to pat down his hair, but he pulls away fast and then rubs his head with both hands. "Yeah, I suppose I am hungry," he says. "Why, what kinda slop we having for dinner, anyhow?"

"What do you like to eat?" I ask. I figure I don't want to stay in on a nice snowy night. Maybe go out and buy something with some of my loot.

"Oh, I dunno. Pizza if you have it. Maybe meatless submarine sandwiches."

"How about a hamburger or Kentucky Fried Chicken, or something like that?" I ask.

"I like them okay, but I don't eat them."

"Why not, you allergic to it?"

"No," he shrugs. "I'm a vegetarian. Sort of."

"A what? Of all the things in the world, you gotta turn out to be an earthy crunchy! What the hell am I supposed to feed you—mashed potatoes and carrots? I bet this ain't even your own idea. What kinda stuff they teachin' you in school, anyhow?"

"It isn't school. It's my mother."

"Whatever. Now, you can be a vegetarian if you want. But if the only food around has meat, then you either eat it or go hungry, you hear?"

*   *   *

Before we even get to the corner of my street, he stops and looks at me. "Do you really think we should be outside? What if somebody sees us?"

"So they see us, we ain't committed any crime," I says. "At least, not that they know about."

"But—if somebody tells my parents, I am compost."

"Nobody's gonna see you. Believe me, nobody, 'cause there's no reason to notice you more than any other kid. Besides, if you want to be out here, this is probably gonna be the last chance."

I don't dare tell him I'm just as nervous. I tell him to stick by me in the city, 'cause I'm a little afraid he could get lost. We come down from Washington Street toward the Faneuil Hall marketplace. Lots of good eating places down there. Kid keeps stopping at the windows in Filene's and Macy's and all, like he never seen them before. Now it's sort of cold, and the kid has nothing for his hands, so I stop at one of the street vendors and get him a pair of real neat gloves with some thick fleece lining inside.

We pass by the old State House with the lion and the unicorn on the roof, and right there is the nut guy. He's got hot almonds and cashews roasted in syrup, and the smell is rich. Then we go through a draft of warm air coming up the stairs of the subway station. Once we get around the corner, the wind whips up like an icy hurricane. We're both covering our eyes as we cross the street for the marketplace.

We eat at Durgin Park, a place they cook all kinds of old New England stuff like Boston baked beans, clam chowder, stuffed lobster, roast turkey. It's upstairs on the second floor, and the windows look out on the marketplace below, all paved with granite and bricks. The trees are decorated in white lights and people are shopping all over. The way they sit you here is at long tables, and before you know it you're sharing the ketchup with other people like it's some kind of church picnic. Gabriel goes right after his corn bread. He slices it in half and tries to butter it, only the butter is hard and he's making a mess. He drops the knife down and pushes the plate away.

"Hey, take it easy there," I says real softly. I pick up the knife and shave small pieces off of the butter and smooth it on my corn bread nice and slow. "Do it easy and you don't have to fight it," I says, and I give him mine. "Whatta you want, better than that?"

"Don't you want it?"

"Sure," I says. I take his and fix it the best I can, and then we both sit there chewing on corn bread and looking at each other. For supper he gets a thing called Bale of Hay, which is all kinds of vegetables done up together. He likes that okay, so he eats hearty and seems to forget he's kidnapped.

"You know, you're the only person I know who doesn't have a telephone," he says. "We have two lines plus a cable modem for computer and fax. And both my parents have cell phones. How do you get by without even one phone?"

"I just do," I says. "If I need to call somebody, I use a pay phone."

"What if somebody wants to call you up?"

"Oh, they just find me. My friends know where to find me."

"I have a friend like that," he says. "He's actually my best friend, and his name is Justin, and he almost always knows where to find me. One time I was picking up the phone to call him, and sure enough, there he was at the kitchen door. Another time I promised him I would share a Sky Bar with him, because that's his totally favorite candy. So I was in the store and bought one, and then I turned around and he was standing right there."

"What do you know—truth is stranger than fiction," I says. "You don't expect him to come poppin' in here right now, do you?"

"Tonight? No, he's in the Christmas Revels. They have rehearsal every day till like night time. He's a boy soprano. He came from England when he was nine, and back there he used to sing in King's College choir. Lots of kids here used to make fun of him because of his accent, but one day he just took a tizzy fit and beated up this kid that was bigger and gave him a bloody nose, only the kid gave Justin a black eye. He didn't care too much, though, because everybody thought he was tough after that."

I find myself smiling, though I don't know if it's because of his story or because of him. "How does a nine-year-old kid go to college?" I ask.

"Oh, you're way behind," he says. "You don't even have a CD player, so how would you know? It's one of the British choir schools, and they accept boys from age seven."

"Well, wait a minute. I'll just go buy a CD player, and then I'll know everything there is to know," I says.

He looks at me, then says, "You're weird."

After we eat, we go around from store to store, that's what the kid says he wants to do—look at the toys. Then we pass through the center market building, and they got this partridge in a pear tree contraption set up inside with all kinds of money getting tossed in by visitors. The kid gets real excited, he stops and looks, then arches his head way back to look up into the blue roof dome. He says, "Let's go upstairs!" and before he even takes his next breath he's running up the stairs to the top level, and I'm hustling right after him. We stand at the railing, and I watch him soaking up the whole place with big eyes—first looking at the pear tree scenes, then gawking up at the roof dome, then watching the crowds milling up and down the stairs. When we get back downstairs, he goes over to the bakery counter and then to the candy apple counter where they got those caramel and coconut apples on a stick. Kid touches everything, he's always with his fingers into stuff. He starts on the apples, and I go up to him and pull his hand down. "Hey," I says, "get your grubs offa things don't belong to you."

"Aw shoot, you're just like my mother. Don't touch this, don't touch anything," he says, then sticks his hands in his pockets.

"Where's the new gloves I bought?"

"Right here," he says, and pulls them out of his coat.

"Okay. Now just be careful of what you touch."

He keeps looking over to them pretty girls behind the taffy apple counter. There's music playing all around and bells ringing, and the air is full of gingerbread and sweet smells. I says to myself, aw let the kid. He's only a kid and he don't see the point in acting adult. Besides, he ain't going to be able to do all this when I start dickering for the ransom. So I pull out three bucks and tell the girl to give the kid one of them apples.

Later on, we're outside by the Christmas trees. The kid hands me the apple with a few bites chewed out crooked because of his missing tooth. "Want some?"

"No, no—you have it."

"I'm kind of full."

I take the apple and try a bite, and it's really good.

"Hey Mister," he says, "can I ask you something?"

"Like what?" I says.

"Are you gonna skip getting a tree this year, too?"

"What do you mean by that?" I ask.

"Well, are you going to get one, or are you going to not?"

"What do I want a thing like that in my house for?" I ask. "I ain't got any lights or stuff."

Kid's full of questions, and pretty personal, too. Why don't I buy some, how come I don't bother, nice smell like that should clear the stale smell in the apartment, personal stuff like he has no business sticking his little nose in. "Let's buy one," he says. "It isn't far to carry it anyhow. Come on."

If it's going to keep him quiet and cooperative, I think, why not pick one and drag it home and keep the little snipe busy while I'm out playing Santa Claus. The kid wasn't any trouble to me so far. So I says, "Okay, go pile in and see which one is the best."

Crazy kid is happy as can be, big fat grin showing his missing tooth, and them brown eyes twinkling up at me. "Thanks!" he says, and runs through all the rows of trees, like a puppy dog or something.

I can't figure it. Something is kinda fishy in Denmark. I pick up this kid who don't know me and who never seen me before, and kidnap him. Then I tie him to a chair and he unties himself, but instead of hitting the road, he goes to take a nap. And now he wants to buy a Christmas tree for my place.

\* \* \*

When we get home, Gabriel tells me I should go out shopping in the morning to find some stuff to hang on the tree. "And a stand to hold some water," he says. Kid is pretty smart, I would've never thought of that.

"Okay," I says. "I'll go and get some stuff to keep you busy, but you'll have to stay chained inside."

He gives me a funny look. "Chained?" he says.

I pull this small link chain from under the couch and show him. "It won't hurt you, but you gotta keep it on all the time from now on."

"Like fun it won't hurt me—just because you don't have to go around all day with a leash around your neck like some mad ass junkyard dog."

"Not your neck, your ankle. And watch the smarty mouth. Your ankle, okay?"

"Then what if I have to go to the bathroom?" he says.

"It's plenty long enough, see?"

"So, how come I can't just go to the window and scream out for somebody to call the cops?" he says.

"Because, wise guy. If you do then it's bye-bye to the both of us." And I make a finger across my neck to show him just what I mean.

He don't say a thing, he just stands there in the den kind of dumb and sad looking while I lock the chain around his ankle, and then lock the other end to the heat pipe that goes through the corner of the room to upstairs. I go and get a couple blankets for him and a pillow, set them up nice on the couch for him to sleep on.

"Here's your bed," I says. He looks at me with them eyes again, then sits down on the couch. Then he gets up and goes over to where the Christmas tree is leaning in the corner. He starts playing with the branches, smelling them and stalling like I wasn't even there.

"Well, ain't you gonna go to sleep?" I ask. "It's almost ten o'clock."

"Maybe in a while," he says.

"You say your prayers, kid. Don't forget to say your prayers before you go to sleep."

"I don't say prayers."

"What do you mean you don't say prayers?" I ask.

He shrugs.

"Well I'll be. Name like Gabriel? That's the name of an angel, you know."

"I don't know any. I knew a couple of short ones my grandmother taught me when I was little, but I forgot them. We're not a very religious family."

"Well, I'll teach you one. What happens if you got sick and died, anyhow? Ever think about that?"

Gabriel sits down again. "Sometimes I think about it and get sort of scared."

"That's 'cause you don't know what to do after you die.

Me, I'm goin' to heaven. So I ain't too scared. I suppose I'll have to burn a little before the time, anyhow."

"Burn! How come?" he asks me.

"Boy, are you a tough case. Don't you know you got to pay for havin' bad ways?"

"Will you teach me some prayers?"

"Sure, I'll teach you. Every night at bedtime you say, 'Now I lay me down to sleep, I pray the Lord my soul to keep. And if I die before I wake, I pray the Lord my soul to take.'" It don't take the kid too long to learn it. He's pretty smart and that's good, because I'm too tuckered out to give lessons anyhow.

I go in my bedroom and start to undress for bed, then when I'm all set and said my prayers, I see the light still on in the den. I go back to see the kid still sitting on the couch.

"Ain't you tired?" I ask.

"Sure. I just don't have any stuff to sleep in."

"You got blankets, don't you?"

"I mean pajamas," he says.

"Oh, for cripes sake, just sleep in your underwear like I do. Go ahead, get to sleep."

"Then, how am I supposed to get undressed if I have this chain on?"

"Oh shoot, I forgot." I undo the lock around his leg and see his pants legs are still wet from walking in the snow. I think, how come I didn't notice that while I was putting the chain on? I let him get out of his wet stuff, then I put it all on the radiator to dry overnight. I tell him, "I'll pick up some pajamas for you tomorrow. Now get to sleep."

"Aren't you going to put the chain back on?"

I pick up the chain and lock it back around his ankle.

# TAPE THREE

Next morning the kid is sound asleep when I get up. I figure it's a good time to get a bath, since I didn't take one yesterday. First I start shaving, then I run some steaming water in the tub. While I'm waiting for that, I check on the kid and he's still sleeping. I put on some coffee water so that it'll be ready.

Top half of the bathroom window you can see through, but the bottom is frosted glass. Out the top I see the sky moving all around gray and angry like, and looking like it's ready for more snow. Good, I think. Snow makes all the folks down town happy to drop a few bucks for Santa Claus. All the while I take a bath and dry off and find some warm stuff to wear under my Santa suit, I keep trying to figure out how to get in that suit and then out of it without going down the cellar. Once I'm dressed, I measure some seeds in the coffee pot, and that's perking all over the stove until I get the cover on. Then I turn the radio on low. I hear Gabriel start to move in the den.

I walk in the den and see him sitting there in his under-wear and a T-shirt, kind of crying and kind of scared. "What's the matter, kid?" I says. "You have a bad dream?"

He looks down at himself and then back to me. "I—I wet the bed," he says.

"For cripes sake!" I start to yell, but then I see the kid sitting there crying. "Okay, okay. What happened, you dream about peeing or something?" I ask, trying not to get too mad. Kid peed on my couch.

"No," he says. "I was kind of cold and I do it a lot of times, anyway. I can't help it."

So this is what I get, I think. But then—so what the hell. Better the kid pees on the old shaggy hulk than he tries to run away and put the finger on me. He's only a kid, anyhow.

I undo the chain and tell him to go and take a hot bath. He changes out of his wet stuff and puts a towel around himself, then takes a bunch of paper towels and blots them over the couch. Next thing I know, he's taking off the blankets. He piles them in the middle of the kitchen floor, then adds all his clothes.

"What's all that for?" I ask.

"So you can take it to the laundry. I noticed you don't have a washer and dryer—"

"Oh—yeah. Shove it all in the pillowcase."

He packs all the stuff in the pillowcase, then goes back in the den and takes the paper towels off of the couch and throws them away. It feels awful strange having a kid traipsing around my apartment, tidying things up and not knowing much about me at all.

"Want some coffee before your bath?" I ask him.

"Ahm—I don't drink it," he says.

"Then some milk? I got some Wheaties and Cap'n Crunch if you want them."

"Okay," he says, and we sit down to breakfast just like we always known each other.

"Hey, tell me one thing," I says. "How come you don't try to take off?"

"I don't know," he shrugs, looks away from me. "How can I? I don't even have my clothes to put on. What am I supposed to do, go out like this?"

I see he ain't coming up with the whole answer. "But how come you don't just slip in your clothes and sneak out?"

"You told me not to try anything."

Well, I think, that sounds more like it. Still seems to me the kid ain't so dumb. What could I do if he just up and took off? I ask him again if that was really why.

"I don't know," he says again. "Then I'd have to go to school and that's boring, and home is boring, too. There's not so many kids and besides, I don't like it there."

"Nice home like yours? What'sa matter with you?"

He looks down at his dish and don't say any more. If I was that kid, I'd have been gone yesterday, right back home. I tell him so, too, and make him think about it.

He says, "Well, it was you that did the freakin' crime anyway, wasn't it? I would've been home."

Now I'm so flabbergasted I don't even reach over and swipe the kid for cussing. And I don't flabber easy. "Oh really?" I says. "Don't be so sure. What if you got picked up by some serial killer? You ever stop to think about that?"

He looks down at the milk in the bottom of his bowl for a long time, and then he looks at me. Nobody says a word. I see I made him scared, way too scared for a kid who's been trying to make me think he's so tough. "You know," I says, "what I'd like to know most of all is, how come you were out there hitch-hiking in the first place?"

He gets this look on his face, all gloomy and cloudy like, then he takes a long breath. "Because I felt like it, okay?"

"Sure, sure. But why did you feel like it?"

"They never let me do anything," he says. "I hate them."

"Like what don't they let you do?"

"For example, a fake Christmas tree. I made a voodoo doll of Martha Stewart and hung it from the neck on the back of the tree, then she found it and I got a big call down because it was supposed to be disrespecting my mother."

"Oh stop it, kid. That ain't even close."

He stands up, kind of mad now. "Well if you really want to know, they wouldn't let me go on the big Polar Sleepover that I was looking forward to since last year. That time the excuse was I was too young, even though I was ten and a lot of the kids were nine. So I waited and waited for this year to come, and then my mother said she thought it might be nice, but my father nixed it."

"How come? Did you do something bad?"

"I don't know. He always says, 'This isn't punishment, Gabriel.' Oh, just forget it. I don't care."

"Sounds like you do care."

"So, now I'm here and you're not hurting me any. I just figure I may as well stick around, see what happens."

"Cryin' out loud, I don't understand you at all. Go on, sit down and finish your breakfast and have your bath. I'm gonna go do the laundry and get some stuff for you."

"Aren't you going to use the chain?"

I look at the kid for a long time, and he looks at me, too. "Just stay there, it reaches," I says.

# TAPE FOUR

It sure takes a long time to get through the morning. First I go in the laundry and get Gabriel's clothes started. While that's doing, I go down to the store and buy some things for his Christmas tree. Inside the store they have all kinds of trees set up, all fake, and each one has a different style of decorations. One is done in all red, white and blue. I'll be pecked if any-body'd put that in their house—except some politician, maybe.

I buy some tinsel and a bunch of boxes of the fanciest bulbs they have. Some look like apples and pears, and some are glass with the nicest pictures, say 'hand painted in Italy,' and cost pretty much, too. I figure I got to get quality things. Some folks buy junk and let it go. I don't want the kid to think I buy junk. They got lots of lights too, and I buy miniature ones in different colors. The back of the box says you need six for a seven foot tree, so I get six. Then after I pay for everything and I'm about to head out, I remember about the water stand. I tell the lady to hang on a second, I have one more thing. Nice lady, she smiles and says, "You just go ahead and help yourself."

Now that's all taken care of, thank goodness. With this

great big bag I head on to the department store, pick up the kid some new underwear, size twelve like he says, and a real fancy pair camouflage pajamas made out of that fluffy flannel stuff. For a guy I do all right buying clothes.

I pass by this church on the way back, figure I might stop in and visit. It has that mellow old church smell inside. I sit down on an oak bench that creaks a little, put my bags next to me as I look around. Only two people inside—some lady up near the candles praying, and me.

I says, "Jesus, I know I ain't no big prize. I don't know what to do about that Gabriel kid. He peed on my couch. I don't care about that so much, but can you give me some ideas?"

Well, Jesus don't always answer too fast, so I just figure I might help it along. I go out and walk about town waiting for an answer, and what do I see, a drug store. I go in and says to the guy at the counter, "Do you have any kind of a pill or something for a kid wets the bed at night?"

"Sure I do," the guy says. He asks me all these questions about the kid and I get the willies for a while. They're pretty personal questions, and I don't know Gabriel too good.

I says, "Just give me the easiest thing."

He puts a couple things on the counter and says, "This is a box of bed liners. They work fine as long as they're under the sleeper. A disadvantage is that they get moved around. Now these," he says as he points to another box, "are called Good Nites. There are fourteen to a box and they're very absorbent, and can be worn under clothing. Very convenient."

"But the kid's eleven years old. He ain't gonna wear no baby diaper stuff!"

"These come in all sizes, and people of all ages use them. It's the best I can do, unless you want to order that electric alarm set."

I think about that a while. He says it's safe, but I don't want the kid to shock himself to death for just piddling the sheets, in case there gets to be a broken wire or something. I seen them news stories about shocking mental people. I just says, "No. Just give me the Good Nite things and let it go."

By then the laundry is done. I go in and pack up for home with the most bundles I ever remember lugging since I moved to Boston after the breakup.

\* \* \*

I don't have the heart to tell the kid about the diapers when I first get in. I figure just show him one easy at night and then he won't get too uppity.

I show him the bag full of all the decorations, and he goes for it just like I figured he would. I pull it away and says, "Oh no. Clothes on first." I unlock his chain and give him the bag with the new underwear and new pajamas in it. When he opens it up he looks at me real happy, then he's just about to strip the towel off of himself and remembers he's in front of a stranger. He turns his back on me and puts on a new pair of drawers. Then instead of putting on his pants, he puts on the new camouflage pajamas.

"Hey, these are way cool," he says, all excited. He pats down the front of the shirt and looks at himself standing there, then he looks at me with them bright eyes again like he does so often.

"Whatta you want, better than that?"

"Now all I need is a paintball gun."

"You ain't gettin' any guns, wise guy. Now it's daytime, so why don't you put on some regular clothes?"

"But I'm staying inside, can't I just keep them on?"

I look at him. "Okay, you can keep them on. Now, lookit what I got here." I show him the bag with the decorations.

"Hey! You got the stand, and lights and bulbs—wow, those are beautiful," he says. "Help me put the tree in the stand so we can decorate it."

"We?" I ask. "I can't do that stuff, I gotta get out and work. You can do it."

"All by myself? It's more fun if we both do it, don't you think?"

"You ain't here for no fun," I says. Then I says, "Oh, all right, all right. Just do some while I'm out, then when I come back to supper you can have me to help you."

"No."

"No what?"

He stands there and looks up at me. "I'll wait till you come home so we can both do it all."

"I gotta go out tonight."

"You won't even be in for an hour?" he says sad like, and he looks at his feet.

"Sure I will, sure. I guess I can be around for an hour or so."

"Where are you going to go?"

"Out, to work."

"I mean tonight. Do you work at night?"

"No. I'm headin' out to the movies or somethin'."

"With your girlfriend?"

"No," I says. "Not with no girlfriend."

"Oh—don't you have a girlfriend?"

"Hey kid, you ask too many questions," I says. "So just shut up. I gotta get to work now."

"But help me put the tree in the stand, anyway, so I can water it."

I help him with the tree, then when we get it upright so it don't keel over, he stands back and looks at it with a big grin on. He looks at his hands, and they have sap stains on them. He puts them up to my nose. "Smells awesome, doesn't it?" he says.

"Sure." I go in my room and grab my Santa Claus suit and shove it quick in a paper bag, figure I can change in some gas station bathroom. Then I go back in the den and lock the kid to the chain and leave quick, so I don't lose the whole day.

*     *     *

It ain't much trouble for me to find a new place to put on the Santa suit, a public bathroom with mirrors, fourth floor of Filene's. I stick the paper bag with the red cheek stuff under my belt to keep it safe. The day ain't too rich with charity like I thought it was going to be. It's kind of slow all around, probably because of the snow being on the ground and making things slushy. Lots of people out shopping, though. I think maybe the weekend will be better, when people take their kids to town. Kids love to drop money in pots, I see it all the time. Good for them, good for me.

I start wondering about how I'm gonna break it to old Mister Winthrop Booker that I kidnapped his kid. I pick up the newspaper and check all the way through twice and don't see any story about a politician's kid being missing from home. That's it, I think—the old man don't know the kid was stolen. Nobody knows it, not a soul was around but me and the kid anyhow, when it happened. So the old man will have to know the kid was kidnapped before anything goes in the papers. Otherwise, they'll just think he took another powder, and they won't want it in the papers that a big shot's kid runs away from a nice home.

I think some more. Do I send a letter, or do I call on the telephone? If I send a letter, they'll find some fingerprints or something. No, I can wear some gloves. But then, they can never tell if I really have the kid. Phone calls are best—that way I can have Gabriel talk, too.

All the time I'm ringing my bell and calling for charity, coins for the needy. Not too many people pitch in, maybe I ain't ho-ho-hoing too enthusiastically today. I try to do a little better, but still it's pretty slow.

Phone calls are what they use in the shows. I can use a pay phone, that's perfect. I ring the bell some more. All of a sudden I think, how do I get the kid to a phone booth? If somebody sees me rustling the kid up to a phone booth, then that could be the end of the whole affair. I see I'm up a stump now.

While I'm thinking, the art girl comes along with this huge folder she sometimes carries. She's wearing this dark purple quilted coat, and her hair is in about two dozen braids coming down from a neon yellow Indiana Jones type hat. "Ho-ho-ho," I says. "Very nice hat."

"I like yours too," she says and smiles. She's got a little space between her front teeth.

"Say, can I ask you somethin'?" I says.

Her eyebrows go up a little and she stops. "Sure," she says.

"What's better, phone calls or letters?"

She looks at me a while. "What do you mean, like for business or romance?"

"I don't know. Say both."

"Phone calls are good. You can hear things in the voice,"she says. "But letters, I like letters. You can read them again for years."

"I see. Thanks."

"Gotta go," she says, and she gets a grip on her folder. After she takes a couple steps, she turns back around. "Someday I'm going to draw a Christmas card of you."

"Ahm—great. Good night!"

When the sun starts to set, I pack up and head home. I don't want to stay out in the dark, it's too dangerous. Lot of muggers out there. Bad enough in the daytime, but night time is a sure mug. So I go in the department store and slip in a dressing room to change. I stick the money bag in my pants as usual, then pack up the outfit and shove off for home.

\*   \*   \*

Gabriel jumps up when I get inside. "Hey Mister," he says, "I was looking at the decorations in the bags, and I noticed there aren't any hooks to put up the bulbs with."

"Don't bother me now," I says. "Go watch the TV."

He sulks over to the TV and clicks it on, then sits down, rubbing his ankle where the chain is. I go in my room and put away the Santa suit, then I start to undo my pants to get the money bag. All of a sudden I hear the kid walking around with the chain banging and clanking.

"Hey—I thought I told you to sit and watch the TV," I says, clutching my belt closed. He's up to the door of my room and looks right in.

"Can I come in?"

"For what? No, get outa here and get to watchin' the TV or else you're gonna be in trouble. Geez, kid—you give me the jeebies sometimes."

He clanks back to the den. Close call, I think as I wrestle out the money bag. I fumble, and it falls to the floor with a clunk and some of the jingle comes out on the linoleum. I pick it up quick and put it all in my drawer with the other money. I see I got only about thirty, forty bucks today. I wish it didn't fall like that, now Gabriel knows I got money around.

After I'm organized, I go in the den to sit on the couch. Just as I almost touch, I remember I can't. I move down another cushion.

Gabriel turns around from the TV. "Aren't you going to go and buy hooks for the bulbs?" he asks.

"I says don't bother me. Just shut up and leave me think."

"I can go and get them if you want."

I jump up and yell, "No, for cripes sake—will you stop pesterin' me and shut up!" I stamp out of the den and sit at the kitchen table.

Finally, I think of a plan for the ransom, so I ain't too fidgety anymore. I figure later on tonight, I take the kid and chain his leg to my car door inside, then we drive out of town to a phone booth off of the highway somewhere. Then I make him dial home and that's how I get them to know their kid is stolen.

Now just as I sit there, the little snipe comes out of the den again and looks at me. "I thought you said you were gonna decorate the tree when you came home," he says.

This kid don't quit. I jump up and grab him rough by his arms and drag him back to the chair, sit him down real hard in it. "No," I says. "No. I changed my mind and so you can just wait, you hear?"

He sits there real quiet now, only he looks up to me and watches everything I do. I look at him, and all of a sudden his chin starts to quiver a little, and then he starts to cry. I sit down at the edge of the couch and put my head on my hand.

"I sat here with nothing to do all day," he says. "I waited for you to come back so—so, aw forget it." He turns away and keeps rubbing his eyes every once in a while, sniffling quietly.

"So, I'm a little uppity," I says. "You gotta cry about every-thing? What are you, some kinda crybaby? Okay, okay, so I'll go out and get some hooks, is that what you want?"

"Mm-hmmm," he says, still sniffling. "And I forgot to tell you candy canes, too."

"What the hell you think I am, Santa Claus?" I says. I pull on my coat and head for the door.

"No," he says, and folds his arms. "But do I have to always call you Mister?"

"What's so bad about it?"

"Because I know your name is Duncan."

I stop right where I am, because it's the first time I hear him use my name. "How do you know?"

"Just because I found your license."

"Hey—I didn't bring you here to snoop."

"I didn't snoop." He puts his hands on his hips.

"You always snoop."

"You left it on the windowsill in the bathroom."

"Nothin' I can do about it now," I says, glad my Santa ID is in my Santa suit pocket. "Just don't you call my name in public, and I won't call yours. Now I gotta get goin'."

"Aren't you hungry?"

I turn to him. "Kinda. We can eat when I get back."

# TAPE FIVE

O nce our pizza is gone, Gabriel runs in the den and starts
unpacking the decorations. He makes all neat piles of
the different boxes, puts the hooks on the chair where I tied
him up the first day, and puts the candy canes on another pile.

Then he waits. He sees I'm just sitting at the table, so he
comes back and sits down across from me again, jiggling his
knee up and down and shifting his eyes to me once or twice.

Finally I get up and turn on the radio.

He gets up, too. "Got any music CDs?" he says.

"No, I ain't got any," I says. I head for the den and try to
figure out where to start with that Christmas tree stuff.

He follows me in the den and pulls the chair up to the tree.
That chain on his leg starts getting to me. I don't like the
sound of it clanking. I go to my room to get the key, and he
follows me there, too. "You gotta trail me everywhere?"

"No, I was just—"

"Then stay in the den." I rummage around for the key,
then go unlock him.

"Thanks," he says. Kid's awful polite.

"Okay, now I ain't done one of these things in a long time," I says. "Where are we supposed to start, anyhow?"

"I dunno," he says. "Maybe we should start with the lights, see how it looks." He unpacks the lights from the boxes and gets them stringing out all over the den. "Stand up on the chair," he tells me.

I stand on the chair, and he hands me a string. "Now what?"

"Begin on top, then wind it down until there isn't any more left. Then plug in another bunch."

This kid's pretty smart for his age. The lights hook up real easy, around and around. He keeps on telling me what to do, like even them out here, move that there, stuff like that. Finally I get off of the chair and work on the bottom half of the tree.

Now, the kid's got the bulbs open, and he's got hooks all over the place. Crazy hooks come all bunched up and you have to tangle through them to get what you need. By and by the kid steps on a hook and cries out, "Ow, you freakin'—"

"Hey, what'd I tell you about the mouth?" I says, pointing to him. "Why don't you go put on your shoes?"

"I got feet on these," he says, and lifts up his foot to show me the pajama feet.

"Well, they ain't for when you got hooks on the floor," I says, "so just put on your shoes and shut up."

He crams on his shoes, leaves them untied. "I wish we had some nice music instead of that old crummy radio you have. Why don't you go out and buy some CDs?"

"Because, I ain't got a CD player."

"You should just get an MP3 player or an iPod. You can download twelve million songs for like a few dollars a month on computer."

"And what am I gonna do, walk around with the whole

world of music stuck in my ears? That ain't how music is supposed to be. It's supposed to be in the air, so everybody can hear it together."

"You can connect it to speakers, you know."

"Okay, so I should. But I don't."

He gives me a box with the real fancy bulbs inside, all ready with hooks. He tells me to do the same thing with them that I did with the lights, start at the top. I pull the chair over and stand up on it.

Suddenly the lights go on. "I found the plug," he says from down on the floor. "How's it look?"

"I can't see the whole thing yet, but it smells okay," I says. Then I start hanging the bulbs. He puts a bunch more hooks on another box of bulbs, then he helps hang them on the low branches. He's pretty particular about it, and he does a good job all around. He tells me to mix up the different kinds of bulbs so it looks even.

Pretty soon that's done, and he comes out with the tinsel. He dashes it on a few strings at a time, but I just throw it on fast here and there. He starts to laugh.

"Whatta you laughin' at?"

"Look at what you're doing," he says. "Your side looks like a shaggy dog."

"So what do you want outa me?" I ask. "I ain't no interior decorator, you know."

He helps me fix up my side, then gets out the candy canes and soon that's done, too. He packs up all the boxes, piles them all square behind the couch, then he climbs up on the chair and fixes a couple things. At last he gets down and puts the chair back in the corner by the TV. "Whatta you want, better than that?" he asks.

I find myself smiling because he's trying to copy the way I

talk. "Better than that they don't make. Where'd you learn how to do all that stuff?"

"I guess from watching my mom."

"Like a real pro, you are. She show you how to do it?"

"Sort of. I never got to do much for myself, though. That's the first time I ever got to do the whole tree."

"How come?"

"I don't know. My mom said it had to be perfect for company, and I could only do a little. Sometimes they used to have people come in and take pictures for magazines. My dad said we should skip getting a real tree this year because of the forests. I said the trees are cut down already, and we should at least use them, but he said it was the principle of the thing, and besides, it was a fire hazard. Personally, I think my mom just didn't like the needles on the floor. Oh, I don't care."

"I bet you do care."

He looks down at his shoes and shrugs.

"That's really your first try?" I ask. "Pretty good for a kid, I hafta say."

He looks at me and his eyes are all bright and he has a crooked kind of grin on. The lights are twinkling different colors on his face, red and yellow and green, then blue and pink, then yellow and green. I watch him standing there in them camouflage pajamas, looking up at me. "We really should have some music besides the old radio," he says.

I throw my hands up in the air. "Okay, okay. Sometimes you make me creep, you know that? Once you get something in your head, you don't quit."

"But it's a good thing to have."

"I heard you already."

"You want to go out and buy one?"

"Now? I got things to do."

"Like what?"

"Business, for instance. I gotta get out and make a little phone call."

"To whom? I thought you didn't have a girlfriend."

"To whoomm? Kid, you talk too much. Now shut up and listen. What you're gonna do, you're gonna get outa them pajamas and get your regular clothes on."

"You mean I can go out?"

"Yeah, you're comin' with me, but just for a little bit."

"What are we going to do?"

"Make a phone call."

"Oh. What for?"

"Business. Your folks don't know where you are or even if you're still alive. So that's the business. Come on, get dressed."

\* \* \*

The Dodge Dart takes some time to start, and the kid is giving me all sorts of grief about the chain being cold around his leg, and where do I think he's gonna run to anyways, and stuff like that. Finally we're off, heading for the highway. We come across a rest area that has a telephone sign on it, and we stop there. I get out and open the kid's door. "No trouble from you," I says. "You do exactly as I told you." I unlock his leg and we go to the phone booth together.

The kid makes a mistake the first time punching the number, which is good because it gives me time to copy the number on a piece of paper. I take the phone from him and listen, hear it ringing. Someone picks it up, and I feel my stomach twist. "Hello," I says, "Mister Winthrop Booker?"

"Speaking."

"I have your kid here."

"Hello? You found him?" he says. "Did he run away or something? He's been gone since yesterday, and my wife and I have been calling everywhere for him."

"He ain't run away, Mister," I says. "Try this—he's kidnapped."

"Jesus Christ," Booker says. For the longest time there's complete silence. Then he says, "What do you want from me?"

"What do I want from you? Money. Just money—nice and quiet, no fuss."

"Where's the boy? Where's Gabriel?" he asks.

I stick the phone up to the kid's ear and says to him, "Talk to your dad."

"Hi, Dad?" the kid says.

"That's enough," I says, and grab the phone away. "Now you know I got the kid, Winthrop Booker. Here's what I want from you. No trouble, just pack up one hundred thousand dollars and I'll tell you where to bring it in two days. Get all the cops you want, but it's the green stuff that's gonna get the kid back."

"Two days? Why not earlier? Is the boy okay?"

"Yeah, he's okay. But he won't stay that way unless you get that money up. You got the word." I hang up the phone on him.

\*   \*   \*

Gabriel don't talk much on the way home. While I'm driving I see a shopping center, pull in and stop the car. "Wait right here," I says.

"So, what else can I do?" He kicks his feet and jiggles the chains.

I get out of the car, run in the store. When I come out, I

have this big heavy box, plus a bag. All that stuff I put in the trunk, so the kid don't see what it is.

"I know what it is," he says.

"What?"

"It's a stereo, isn't it? And you also bought some music, didn't you?"

"How did you know?"

"Because."

My throat gets tight. "You got outa this car to spy? I told you to stay here." I grab him by his coat and says, "Look, when I tell you to do somethin' you do it. I ain't playin' games with you."

"Duhh, you left the key in the lock," he says, holding it up for me to see.

"So I did. Don't you know it's bad for you to be out here with people around? What if somebody you know was out there? They could reckonize you, and that'd be the end for the both of us. And don't forget that. From now on you listen good when I tell you somethin'."

"It's bad for you to be out here too, you know. My father has ways to trace that call."

"Whatta you mean? I wasn't on the line long enough."

"Oh, go back to the seventies," he says. "Ever hear of 'star six-nine'? Well, that can tell the number that just called you. And for your information, he's got caller I. D. There's probably at least ten state police at that phone booth by now."

"You really think so? Well, for your information, smarty pants, I know about caller I. D., and it only taps about seventy percent of the calls. That means if your old man pays ten bucks for the service, he's only gettin' seven bucks worth of goods. And it also means you only got seventy percent chance of finding a cop near that phone booth."

"Oh, yeah?" he says. "So then I dare you to drive by it!"

I feel myself kind of mad, and I drive around and head all the way back to the pay phone where I called his father. There ain't a soul to be seen. We head back to the apartment, and this time the kid don't say anything at all.

\*     \*     \*

I get him ready for bed and chain his leg, then I set up the new stereo. It's a pretty good set, with the CD and tape player and an AM/FM receiver and two speakers. Right off I play a tape with Christmas music. I sit down in the chair I used for tying the kid to, and listen to the music and watch the tree. Gabriel's sitting on the couch. I start to get some mixed up feelings, looking at that tree. I seen lots of trees with lights, and heard lots of music almost as nice as what's on, but in my own house it's different. I look at Gabriel, and he's watching the tree, hair coming down his forehead and around the tops of his ears like one of them Christmas card angels you see in the stores.

"Hey, Mister," he says.

"What."

"I thought you were going to a movie tonight."

"So did I," I says. "I already seen most all the shows, though. Sometimes I see two, three in one day. So if I skip it, it don't bother me."

"Oh." He sits quiet a while. Then he says, "You hungry?"

"Yeah, I kinda am, why?"

"Me too."

"Why didn't you say so?"

"I dunno."

"You like crackers with peanut butter and jelly?" I ask. "That's all I got, I have it all the time for a snack."

He smiles and says, "Sure." We munch for a while, and pretty soon the tape is played out.

"Time for you to go to bed," I says. Then I remember what I had to get. I get up and go in my room and open up the box of them Good Nites the drug store guy gave me. I take one in the den and show the kid. "Here," I says. "I got you somethin' for tonight. It's if you wet the bed again, then you won't spoil the couch or your new pajamas."

"What is it?"

"Well, the drug store guy says it's accident proof underwear. It's made special for bigger kids, so in case they have trouble or somethin'—you know."

"All it is is a diaper," he says, and he pushes it away from me. I knew it, I figured this was gonna happen.

"Okay," I says. "I get you a tree and some music and all, so you can keep busy. The least you can do is try to help not spoil my couch."

"I won't spoil it," he says. "I was cold last night because I had no pajamas. I'll be warm tonight—"

"Hey," I says, chopping the air with my hand. "Wear this thing anyhow, because I asked you to and it's my house."

"So, it's not my fault I'm here!"

I almost swipe the kid and he shuts his eyes and pulls his head back scared, but then I just touch his face instead. "I want you to wear it, okay? Don't give me trouble, just wear it."

His face goes red, and he's breathing like a steam radiator, trying not to cry. "I'm not going to wear a diaper."

"Look, it ain't no shame to wear this. See, it says 'Good Nites, sixty-five to eighty-five pounds.' You ever see a sixty-five pound baby? No, 'cause these aren't for babies, they're for regular kids just like you. It's only you and me here and nobody's ever gonna know. It's really just underwear."

"So it's diaper underwear, and I'm not wearing it!"

"Okay, smart guy. Just don't ask me to get you anything more, 'cause I've had it. You know what? Why don't you just pack up your stuff. Go ahead, get your stuff. I'm gonna drive you home right now. This ain't worth any amount of money."

He looks at me like I was a Mack truck ready to mow him down. His face turns fish belly white, and he stands there for a long frozen minute. Then he reaches out his hand and grabs the thing out of my hand. "Okay, I'll wear it. But I won't like it."

"Let me know when you're ready for sleep," I says, and I leave the room for him to change.

# TAPE SIX

Next morning I wake up to the sound of the chain clinking all around. I get up and go in the den. The kid is standing in the middle of the floor with this big huge grin on his face. He looks down at himself and then he goes to his blankets and says, "I'm not wet!"

"So what?" I says.

He looks at me. "I dunno," he says. "Look out, I have to go." He runs past me and does what he has to, then comes right back in with the diaper thing in his hand, tugging on his pajamas like he's real proud of something. "What's for breakfast?" he asks, and he folds the diaper and stuffs it in the trash. Then he looks at the Christmas tree, fixes a bulb, and goes to the stereo and sticks in one of the new tapes.

"I dunno about you, kid. What's got into you today?"

"Nothing, I'm just in a good mood."

"Well that's good," I says. "I'm gonna get some scrambled eggs with toast, you want some?"

"Sure."

"Then get washed up and comb your hair."

"You got a toothbrush?"

"Yeah, I got a few extra ones. They're all new—I got them at the Brooks going out of business sale. Lotta nice soap there, too." I take out a few different color toothbrushes and let him pick the one he wants, orange with gold sparkles.

"Thanks," he says, and clunks toward the bedroom.

"Here, come here kid. Let me take that chain off of you before it makes me nutty." I unlock the chain and he rubs his foot and then goes in to wash. When he comes out, his face is all shiny and he still has a grin on like he just got kissed by Tinkerbell.

I'm cooking the coffee and some scrambled eggs, and Gabriel comes over and watches. "You know," he says, "you should clean up this place. You need a new rug in the den and in your room, too."

"Hey, hey—this ain't a hotel. Whatta you think I am, Rockefeller?"

"And look at the floor. I betcha you didn't wash it for three months."

"Wrong. I clean this floor the end of every month, when the super comes around to clean the hallways."

"Well, under the sink over there looks pretty ripe," he says, pointing.

"Whose house is this, anyhow?" I ask. "Now go sit down if you want to eat."

Just then the toast pops up and the kid runs and butters it, then chops it in half, corner to corner, and puts it on the table. You'd think he was a professional, some of the things he knows. Funny, I always cut the toast that way at the Towne Diner, but I'd never expect a kid to do it.

"It's Saturday, you know," he says when we're eating. "Next Saturday's Christmas."

"Don't remind me," I says.

"Why?" he asks, and I tell him because I'll be out of a job come Christmas.

\*　　\*　　\*

The morning *Herald* has the kid's picture splashed all over it. The headline says, "AMBER ALERT!" Hot damn, I think. Now I'm glad I put that chain on his leg before I left. I'm reading the story and it says, "Gabriel Booker, the only child of State Representative Win Booker, was apparently kidnapped Thursday, it was disclosed yesterday by police." It says there don't seem to be any leads or motives yet, but police are investigating a ransom call allegedly made from a pay phone in an undisclosed location. "However," it says, "the missing child was last seen in a local convenience store, according to the owner Dipesh Patel, who said, 'I know that boy, he comes in all the time. But this time he stayed until after the school bus left. I think he ran away from home.' Police are treating the case as an abduction, and anybody with information is asked to call the State Police Crimestoppers Unit, or the National Center for Missing and Exploited Children." Then they have a separate section about missing children in Massachusetts, and another section on crime prevention.

At least the kid won't see the newspaper, I think. It takes me a long time to get my mind off of that stuff, and the way I finally do it is to remember how the kid was hitchhiking, and how he warmed his hands over the defroster vents.

I see right away it's a good day for Santa Claus and charity. Everybody's passing by and dropping coins and bills for the needy. "Merry Christmas," I says to them all, and I try to mean it the best I can. All morning I stay worried, though. I'm getting the idea I put myself in the same boat with them miserable lowlifes that hurt or murder kids, and every parent that reads the papers today will be having less holiday spirit because of me.

Just about lunch time I see old Dick Murphy come up the street again. He stops and says, "Hello there, old pal Santa Claus Wagner! You know, I forgot to ask you where you're staying these days."

"Oh, I got a little apartment on Carmody Street," I says. "But I don't know how long I'll be there."

"I see. Well, I was thinking we ought to get together some time, have a few beers or something."

"Ahm—I dunno."

"Tell you what—I'll be stopping by the grocery store tonight, why don't you join me? You can drop up after and have a steak or something."

"Right now I don't need much, Murph. You know."

"Oh come on. You look like you need a lot. A lot of somethin' I can't give you."

I laugh, thinking it's just like him. "Maybe another time," I says. "Why don't we make it some night next week, okay?"

"How's Wednesday? My girl usually works Wednesday night."

It feels strange to think of us actually going somewhere, trying to come up with stuff to say. "I dunno," I says. "What do you think?"

"Of course. You can meet me at the Blue Lantern, work your jaw over a couple pops. Listen, this place has pizza, cooked stuff, the works. Let's do it."

"Sure—sure thing, Murph. See you at the Blue Lantern then, about nine or so, okay?"

"Nine is good—till then, pal."

*   *   *

It's a good thing I got on my big pair of pants, I think as I start home at supper time. They're pretty heavy with today's cash. I stop in the gas station bathroom, wash off the extra red on my face and change to my regular clothes, then push on home.

I go in my apartment real quiet, just in time to see the kid coming out of my room. "What were you doin' in there?" I ask.

"Nothing much—just fixing up a little."

I go in my room and shove the Santa suit bag under the bed. I notice the kid made my bed, fixed up stuff all over. I turn around and there's the kid in the doorway, looking at me with eyes like pinwheels.

"You have a lot of money in that drawer, you know," he says.

I don't know whether to swipe him or what. "Look, I don't want you goin' in my stuff, you hear? It's personal, so you just keep your grubs off."

"You should put it in the bank."

"Yeah. Now go in the den, play some of them tapes I got you." He goes, and I hear him in the den so I know it's safe. I take out my money and dump it in the drawer with the rest of the loot, then I fix my pants and head for the den.

Now I see the kitchen floor is all clean, too. "Hey kid," I says. "What?"

"What'd you do, wash the floor?"

"Yeah, you like it? I wasn't doing anything anyhow."

"Ahm, yeah—looks good. Did you eat lunch?"

"Yeah, I had a couple of peanut butter and banana sand-wiches. What's for dinner?"

"I dunno. Spaghetti maybe. I make that pretty good—you like it?"

"Sure do. But no meatballs for me."

I get the kid watching Bugs Bunny while I make supper.

Kid's got some laugh, nice to hear. He sounds tickled when he laughs. While we eat, I tell him he done good with the cleaning up. "You know kid," I says, "whoever marries you is gonna be one lucky girl."

"Hey, Duncan?"

"Yeah?"

"Can I ask you something?"

"Depends on what it is," I says.

"Well, could you call me Gabriel instead of kid?"

"I thought you didn't like the name."

"I didn't used to," he says. "But I guess it sounds kind of okay."

# TAPE SEVEN

Sunday morning I get the sun right on my face about nine, and I wake up. I pull on some pants, then I go in the den to check on the kid. I see the blankets all in a tangle around the couch and floor, and I see he wet again in his sleep. Nothing got on the couch like the first night. I guess them diaper things work okay.

After I unlock his chain, he gets up and has a bath. Then he dresses up and busts into the kitchen. "Sorry I wet the bed again, Duncan. I washed my pajamas and they're hanging over the bath to dry," he says, sitting down.

I get him the Cap'n Crunch and some milk, and put on a pot so I can have coffee.

"Hey, Duncan?"

"What?"

"Will you get mad if I ask you something?"

"No, why—do I get mad when you ask me things?"

"Well, I was wondering. Were you really going to take me home the other night?" He pours out the Cap'n Crunch and it overflows his bowl and dumps all over the table, and he cracks up laughing.

I'm laughing too, and I look in his eyes and they're sparkling. "Yes, Gabriel, I was just about to throw you in the trunk and dump you off home."

He starts to pick up the cereal and fumbles it back into the box bit by bit, stuffing some into his mouth in the meantime. Finally he gets every piece off of the table. He reaches for the milk, but he don't pour it. Now, he looks at me completely straight-faced. "Do you think I'll be able to go home in time for Christmas?"

"I guess so—depends on if it all works out."

"Good, because I'm starting to really miss it. My mom would be making cookies today, and Justin and I would probably be helping decorate them. And then—"

"Oh, so your mom does let you do stuff."

He shrugs. "I guess she does, sometimes."

"What's Christmas like in your family?" I ask.

"Well, it's absolutely, positively my favorite day. I'm usually the first awake, and I run downstairs to the great room where we have the tree, and practically can't get into the room for all the presents. Then we all open our presents, and afterwards we have my mom's Christmas bread for breakfast. Later on my grandmother and my cousins come to visit, and the house is full of people all day, and I'll probably have a total meltdown if I can't be home."

"Well—don't count on it," I says. "Maybe you will and maybe you won't. I'm doin' the best I can."

Even though Sunday's a busy shopping day, I don't go out to play Santa Claus. I like to have a day off—so what if I lose money. For a couple hours we sit in front of the TV, watch a couple old movies on the stations that don't have them church programs on. I'm sitting on the couch where it's not stained, and Gabriel's sitting on the floor on a piece of the rug. By and by a commercial comes on and he gets up. I watch him go in the kitchen, get himself some crackers. He comes back in, gives me half of what he got, then he sits down on the floor again. Only this time, he pulls over to where my feet are, and he sits against my legs.

"This is a real excellent story," he says.

"Yeah, it ain't bad. I usually go up town and see some on the big screens. Sunday's my real show day."

"Why don't you go?"

"Aw, I don't want to have to put the chain on you," I says.

Soon as the movie gets over, the news comes on. Who do we see on it but Mister Winthrop Booker. It ain't so different than any other times because he's always on about affordable housing or the new stadium, or Lottery litter. But this time he's talking about his boy getting kidnapped.

Gabriel sits up straight and moves in front of the TV.

"There's been a demand for ransom," says old Winthrop, "and we're doing all we can to insure the safety of our son." Then the news guy comes in and says, "State Representative Booker has informed police that he refuses to pay the ransom demand. 'Ransom never guaranteed anybody's safe return,' said Representative Booker, and he added the statement, 'I refuse to submit to terrorism and extortion.'" Then the announcer says, "So far, there are no witnesses and no substantial leads to this frightening crime."

I get up and shut the news off. The kid's face is kinda cloudy. "What'sa matter now?" I ask.

"I knew he wouldn't pay," he says, and then he just goes to the couch and lies down, hiding his face.

"He's gonna pay it," I says. "He'll pay it and don't you worry." I feel myself flashing hot around my neck and down my shoulders. I go in my room and pull my coat on. I take the chain and unravel it from the pipe, lock it back up to the kid's leg. "You wait right here," I says. He don't say a word, just stays there with his face buried.

*     *     *

When I get to my car, I see I only have about twenty bucks with me. More than enough, I think, and I pile in and drive out toward the highway. Along the way, I find a phone booth outside a gas station. I know I got the number in my coat somewhere, and fish through all the pockets. Finally I find it and dial. "Mister Winthrop Booker?" I ask.

"Speaking."

"Mister Booker," I says, "I hear you ain't ready to pay up for the kid."

"Look here," he says real mad like, "I won't pay you or any-one of your kind a dime. How do I know the boy is safe?"

"You don't know, but I do."

"Is he there? Is he all right? Put him on."

"He ain't here. He's all right, but he ain't here. All I know is he was watchin' the news and he seen you say you wouldn't pay. You made the kid jumpy, and you made him think you don't care. That ain't too smart, Booker. What's the matter, don't you appreciate havin' a kid?"

He don't say anything.

"I ain't gonna stay on the line," I says. "All I'm gonna say is get that money and pay for the kid."

"I'm not going to submit to your extortion," he says.

"Then do what you will and be damned, you jerky. If you want to see your kid again, just pay," I says, and then hang up the phone hard and go to my car.

*     *     *

I come home good and steaming. Gabriel gets up and clunks the chain through the kitchen to me. "Where'd you go?" he asks.

"Nowhere." I go in my room and take off my coat. He follows me in there with that chain, and he just stands there looking. I feel myself all knots inside, and I bite my jaws together.

"Did you call my house?"

I try to get out of my bedroom door, and he's in the way. "Move outa the way," I says.

"Did you call my house?"

"It's none of your damn business what I did or where I went. Willya just get the hell outa my way!" I says, and I grab him and shove him back before I can even catch myself. He sucks in some air, stands back against the fridge and stares up at me real scared. In a second I see the tears start to come down his face—no sound, just tears running down.

"Oh Jesus," I says. "I'm sorry, kid. I'm sorry, I didn't mean to do that." I put my hand on his head and try to make him stop crying, but he just keeps on.

"What's going to happen to me now?" he says.

"I dunno."

"You did call my house, huhn?"

"Yeah, I called. Seems your old man means it. But, don't you worry, kid. He's gonna pay."

"What happens if he doesn't?"

"I dunno," I says, and I let go of his head. He turns away and goes in the den to sit down.

\* \* \*

The rest of the day he says nothing to me. I turn on the TV, and he turns his head the other way. I put on the Christmas tree, and he looks at the wall instead. So I turn both off and leave the room.

When I go back in, I see the kid's crying again. "Damn you, kid. Will you ever stop your cryin'?"

"For what?"

"There ain't nothin' to cry about, now."

"Not for you," he says. "I'm the one who gets hurt, why should you cry?"

"What hurts?"

"Nothing much—just that you're going to kill me if my father doesn't pay. See how much he cares."

"He'll pay," I says.

"What if he doesn't?"

"He will, for cripes sake, willya stop your blubberin'?"

"How do you know? That's what I want to know, what happens to me if he won't pay?" He's shaking a little, looking at me with scared, wet eyes.

I stand up, feeling the blood run hot in my face. "I'll tell you what's gonna happen if he don't pay for his kid," I says, and I point to Gabriel. "I'm gonna go burn the house down to the ground, and when he comes out of it, I'll kick his ass from here to Minnesota."

Gabriel is still scared, pressed against the end of the couch. "What—what about me?"

"Aw, hell," I says. "Nothin's gonna happen to you."

He gets up off of the couch and clinks the chain across the floor to me, and he puts his arms around my waist and hugs. I put my arms over the kid's back and pat him for a while because I see he's real shook up, and he squeezes tighter, so I hold him tight for a while.

*   *   *

By and by comes supper time, and we eat some vegetable chow mein, only I have a hamburger with mine. While we eat, the kid says, "I wish I could go out afterwards and take a ride or a walk or something."

"I ain't about to mess things up now, kid."

"I thought you were going to call me Gabriel."

"Gabriel, then. If we get caught out there, then that's the end for both of us. Those cops start shootin', and you never know what they'll hit. You wanna go out at one o'clock in the mornin', then that's a different—"

"Yeah, that's okay!" he shouts. "One o'clock, that'll be the latest I ever got to stay up. Can we? Can we go out tonight at one and throw snow or something?"

"Whatta you think I am, a kid?"

"But will you wake me up so I can at least go outside? I wasn't out for two days."

"That's part of gettin' kidnapped, you know."

"We can go for a ride, can't we?"

"I dunno. Maybe, sure."

His eyes are shining now. "When will we go, then?"

"Around ten-thirty or eleven," I says. "Can't stop anyplace where there might be people, though."

After we eat, we go to watch some more TV. *Mister Magoo's Christmas Carol* is playing, and it's kind of sad. When Scrooge is in Christmas past, and his old girlfriend Belle is singing "Winter Was Warm," it makes my throat tight. She says, "Good bye, Ebenezer," but I'm hearing, "Good bye, Duncan," and I have to blink my eyes to keep tears back. Now the kid likes sitting on the floor and leaning on my legs— crazy kid.

\* \* \*

Come about ten, Gabriel starts to get fidgety. He gets his coat all ready, and them gloves with the Polartec fleece inside. He sits on the couch, then he gets up, then he sits down again. By and by he says, "Can't we just go now?"

"Okay," I says. I undo the chain from around the pipe, wrap it up and stick it in a paper bag.

"You going to take the chain?"

"This is a kidnappin', remember?"

We pile in the car and nobody sees us. I keep thinking, what if anyone who saw the news ever sees the kid? After all, his face is all over the nation—anyone can tell if they see him. We ride up and down the highway for half an hour, then we come to a rest stop. I pull the car in and park as far to the back as I can. The kid starts to try the door and gets all tangled up.

"That's my job," I says, and I unlock the chain and let him dis-tangle himself while I go around to open the door. He jumps out of the car and almost falls on a patch of ice. Real quiet he waits, keeping his eyes on me as I close the door. Then he runs away and picks up a hunk of snow and aims it at me. He misses, then gets another one.

"Don't you hit me with them," I says.

"Why not?" he says, and throws another.

"Just don't do it," I says, but it's too late. He lets one splat on my arm and he's laughing. Kid starts to run around like crazy with that tickled laugh of his, and he grabs some more snow. Now I'm after him. I don't know if he's gonna run away to the woods or what. I start to get nervous about that, because he said he wants to be home for Christmas, and he knows his father is kicking up a fuss about paying.

He runs around and around the car, then heads for the snow plowed up at the side of the rest stop. He piles over a snowbank and falls down just as I get to him, and he turns over on his back and looks up at me, laughing and laughing.

"Don't you try that snow stuff again," I says. "And don't you try to run away."

"What if I want to?"

"Then I'll come after you, and the next time I'll put the chain around your neck."

"Oh really?" he says, and he turns over quick and scrambles up. He stands there looking at me, and I see he's got a snowball in his hand. He throws the snow at me and turns fast to run, and he gets away. I run after him, but just as he's near the trees he turns around to see how close I am. Only I'm too close—I tumble into him and take him down in the snow.

Crazy kid is still laughing. "Scared you, didn't I?" he says.

"Yeah, I'm real scared, kid."

"Gabriel."

"Gabriel."

"You think we should get something to eat?"

"You know we can't."

"But—"

"So forget it. Get it outa your mind right now because there's no way you can get seen. That would be so stupid."

"But I'm hungry. Can't you just stop at a pizza shop and get something? Nobody'll see me, just park in the dark."

"I dunno, maybe."

"Want to throw some more snow?" he asks, then he gets up and throws more before I can answer.

"Yeah, I do," I says, and I pick up a bunch and chase him down and throw it. It slaps him right in the back of the leg, and he turns around with another one and hits me right on my coat front. We chase around like that for a while, throwing snow. Then I says, "Let's get goin'. I hafta work tomorrow, and I'm startin' to get wet, anyhow."

"We going to eat somewhere?"

"Didn't you hear me say maybe?" I chain his ankle in the car and drive back on the highway to town.

*   *   *

The worst thing happens.

I'm doing about fifty in my Dart when the back tire blows out. My heart jolts, banging away inside me. I think, this is it for me. Somehow I get the car off on the side of the road, get out and slam the door. I open the trunk and start to pull out the jack and the spare. The spare is as bald as an eagle, but it has air and should hold till I get home.

I go to Gabriel's window and throw the keys to him. "Take that chain offa your legs and stuff it in the bag right now," I says. "And don't try nothin', because I ain't in the mood."

"Are you gonna put on the flashers?"

"Yeah, yeah—keep from gettin' killed," I says, and I start to get in, but the kid leans over and fidgets with my steering stuff. "I can find it," he says, and clicks the lights on.

Suddenly I see some blue lights coming up the highway. My heart stops beating. "Never mind that, just get the chain offa your feet," I says. I can taste something like I'm biting a piece of cold tin foil. It's gotta be the cops after me, I think, and I get ready to head for the woods. Then I remember the kid.

"Hey, you got that chain offa you yet?" I yell.

He opens his window. "I can't find which key," he calls, and hands the bunch out the window to me. I go for the keys and fumble, and they fall in the snow, so I get down and dig for them.

Now the blue lights are right behind me.

"Here's the keys, I got 'em," I says, and I give them to him. "Get that offa your feet, now."

"Which key do I use?"

"This one, stupid! Don't you remember it from the other night, when you unlocked yourself to watch me buy the stereo?"

"I didn't do that," he says, unlocking the chain real quick. "I only said you left the key in, I didn't say I unlocked myself. You're the one who said I got out to spy, not me."

"Then how did you know what I bought?" I ask.

"Duh-hh. What else were you going to buy in a big box like that?" the kid says, and he grins at me and shoves the chain in the bag just as the cruiser pulls to a stop behind my car.

# TAPE EIGHT

I'm about to chew the kid out for grinning at a time like this, but I see I don't have the time. I start to the back of the car and begin to set up the jack.

Cop gets out of his car, walks toward me looking twice as big as Arnold Schwarzenegger. My mouth is alive with an electric taste. My heart is slamming in my chest and neck, but I try to hide it and just kinda keep working on the flat. Step by step the cop comes closer, and suddenly he's standing by my bumper. "Cold night," he says.

"Damn cold," I says, but I don't feel anything except my squirming intestines.

"Everything okay?" he asks.

"Yeah, just gotta get this tire changed and everything'll be fine."

"I'll just hang around here so you can get it done safely," he says. "Need some light?"

"Naw, I got enough now."

It feels like I'm changing that tire ten times in a row with the cop around. He goes back to sit in his car, and I see him pick up his radio and start talking into it. Then I steal a look to see how Gabriel is, and he's sitting there in the car real quiet.

Finally I get the tire changed. I toss the old flat and the jack in the trunk and close it. The cop gets out of his car again and starts walking up to me. I stand there and face him, real full of the willies now. He starts to look over the car.

"Looking for something?" I ask.

"Just checking your tire," he says. "I thought I saw you put only four lug nuts back on."

I go over to the tire with him and he looks at the ground. "There it is," he says, and points to a lug nut on the ground. "Better get that on," he says.

"Oh—" I says, and I go to fish in my pocket for the keys. Then I remember Gabriel has them. I says, "Wait, I gotta get my keys to open the trunk again."

I open the door, and I see the kid clanking through the bag of chains. "Gimme the key, quick!" I whisper. He's still clanking around. "Where the hell are they?" I says, and he looks at me sorta worried.

"They're in the bag with the chain," he says. "Oh, I found them. Here."

I grab them and open the trunk, take the tire iron out and work on the missing lug. Just as I'm putting it on, I notice the cop checking my license plate. I finish up the tire, then throw the iron back in the trunk. "See somethin' wrong?"

"You have to get a new sticker before January, pal," he says. "Your registration runs out at the end of the month—just thought I'd remind you."

"Oh, ahm—good thing you saw it, I sometimes forget about stuff like that."

"Glad I could help."

"Sure. Thanks a lot."

"Have a nice holiday," he says.

This cop is giving me the creeps a hundred miles an hour. I wag my hand in the air and shrug my shoulders. I'm just waiting for him to come out and arrest me, but he don't. I says, "Well—have a nice one for yourself, too."

Next thing I know the cop is gone. I feel so lucky I could scream, but at the same time I feel real mad. I get back in the car. "What took you so long with them keys?"

"I couldn't find them," Gabriel says.

"From now on don't be so damn stupid. Why'd you hafta go and toss the keys in with the chain?"

"You told me to hurry."

"I didn't tell you to be stupid."

"I'm not stupid," he says, "at least I got it off in time. And in case you didn't notice, you're the one that put the cruddy dog butt chain on me in the first place. Besides, I didn't yell for the cop either."

I look at him and think. He's right, he could have caused a lot of trouble. Makes me look like the stupid one. "Why didn't you try and call him, anyhow?"

"I dunno," he says. "I didn't know his name."

"Hey," I says. "Come here."

"I am here."

"Closer."

He edges one inch closer to me, sort of unsure about what I plan. I put my arm over his shoulders and pat him. "Tell me the truth," I says. "How come you didn't try to get away?"

"Are you serious? He was a state trooper, and they have googol caliber guns. If I started screaming and he saw who I was, then he might take out his gun and shoot you or arrest you. That would be bye-bye to the both of us." He cuts a finger across his throat and then drops his head back, with his tongue hanging way out of his mouth.

*   *   *

In the middle of the night I wake up to hear the kid calling me from the den. I turn on my little night lamp, and my eyes go all blind.

"Duncan?"

I get up, stumble into the den to see what's eating him. His eyes get squinty when I put on the light. "What'sa matter?"

"I'm scared."

"You wake me up for that? Cripes sake, kid."

He's got blankets all wrapped up to his neck, and he's sitting on the couch instead of lying down. "I'm scared."

"Well what the hell you want me to do about it?"

"Can I sleep in your room?"

"Are you outa your mind? I only got one bed in there and the floor's cold as all get out. Now just go back to sleep, and you won't be scared anymore."

"Please?" he says, and he stands up with them blankets around him and he comes near me.

"Well where are you gonna sleep?"

"I dunno. There's room on your bed for—"

"Oh, no there ain't."

"Well, I can sleep on the floor. Or, I can take the couch cushions and sleep on them," he says, and he starts to get them before I even tell him he can.

"Okay," I says, "just make it fast. What the hell time is it, anyhow?" I look at the clock and it says one-thirty, so I see it ain't too late.

"You got the key?"

"For what?"

"To undo the chain."

"The chain can reach my room," I says. Then I go back in my room and hear him clanking that thing around as he walks across the kitchen. It sounds so loud in the dead quiet of the night, and for the first time I'm worried somebody else in the building might hear it, even though this is a pretty soundproof old place. I grab the key and unlock the chain from the kid's leg. "Okay. I can't stand the sound anyhow."

Gabriel barrels into my room and sets the cushions out straight, right across from my bed. He gets down on them and fixes himself all up in the blankets. I turn off the light in the den, then come back in the room and almost fall over the little snipe on my way to bed. When I go to shut off my lamp, he tells me to leave it on.

I look at him—he's lying on his back and looking up to me. "No way," I says. "I gotta get some sleep." I shut the light.

"Hey, Duncan?"

"Whatta you want?"

"Thanks for not tying me back up with the chain."

"That's okay, kid."

"Gabriel. Hey, Duncan?" he starts again. "Wanna know something?"

"Like what?"

"Like, I was thinking. You know, even if you never put that chain on my leg, I don't think I'd run away."

"I know," I says.

"How do you know?"

"Come on, Gabriel. How many times did you have the chance to take a powder and you stayed? I ain't stupid."

"Then how come you always put on the chain?"

"Because this is a kidnapping, that's why. Either you do it right, or you don't bother."

"Oh."

I'm almost ready to drift off, and I hear him call me again. "Whatta you want now? I'm tryin' to sleep, for cripes sake."

"How come you don't have a girlfriend?"

"None of your business," I says.

Then he don't say anything. I hear him moving, and I look over. From the outside shadows I see him leaning up on his elbow like he's waiting for something. I lean over to my lamp and switch it on again. "Okay," I says. "Because my girlfriend married someone else, that's why."

"Oh. How come you let her?"

"I didn't let her, she just did. I guess she never really loved me, if you want to know the truth. Sometimes people get ideas in their mind that ain't all true."

"So why don't you get another girlfriend?"

There's not much I can answer to that—I never thought about it. Maybe because I'm used to the way my life is, and for all these years I let that be enough. "I dunno," I says. "Girls you can get plenty, but a girl to be in love with is hard to find."

"Did you have a lot of girlfriends before?" he asks, and he sits up on the couch cushions to listen better.

"Did I ever," I says. "See, I was in the service, and I kept tellin' myself that when I got out I was gonna get a good job and find myself a woman, and live the good life. Once I was out, I went with all kinds o' girls, and we got along fine. Nothin' serious—no broken hearts. Then one day I found the one. There was some kinda magic I felt, not just because she was prettier than the others, but she had somethin' electric that I could feel across the room every time I saw her. So I got it in my mind that we were in love, and maybe we were. Or maybe just I was. Anyhow, I thought nothin' could ever stop it from happenin' just the way I saw it."

"How'd she look?"

"I dunno—blond hair and green eyes, not grass green but like the ocean."

"My mom has green eyes," he says.

"Ahm—yeah. Anyhow, things started to break off when she went away to college. She was pretty old for it, about twenty-four or somethin'. She wrote me one time that she was seein' some other guy and it was nothin' serious, that they were just friends. But it turned out much more serious, 'cause she married him."

"Didn't you try to keep her?"

"Yeah, but some real serious stuff happened to her, and there was nothin' I could do about it."

"Like what?"

"Nothin' you need to know." I lean over and flick off my lamp. "I'm tired, so go to sleep so I can rest."

"But—"

"Forget it, kid. It was a long time ago, and there's nothin' I can do to change it now. Good night."

# TAPE NINE

Monday I wake up with a stiff neck like I slept in a noose. My pillow's gone—I guess it fell on the floor. I creak over to pick it up, and see the kid's already out of his bed. Probably in the bathroom, I think, and I call him. He don't answer, so I get up slow and check his bed to see if he wet it. The couch cushions are dry. I call him again, and still he don't answer.

Suddenly I get an idea why. I jump straight up, and my neck wrenches so bad it rings in my ears. I go in the den and the bathroom and then back in my room, even squinch down to look under my bed to see if he's playing a joke. He's nowhere—not behind the furniture, not in the closets. While I think about any other place he might hide, I see my dresser is a little way open. Now I'm on fire. I run to the dresser and yank open my money drawer. The drawer is empty, there ain't a thin dime inside.

All the worst things are going through my head. The kid must've gone straight home with the money, and he's gonna tell the old man who I am and where to get me. And if I don't end up in jail first, I gotta get out and either find that kid or leave town.

I'm almost ready to go for the kid, but then I think there would be no way to catch up with him. Besides, it would be too dangerous. So, I go in the den and turn on the TV, see if there might be any news about the kid going home. One news station has some talk about Gabriel being sighted on Martha's Vineyard, and how State Police helicopters are flying to the island to investigate. News lady says there have been other sightings of Gabriel in Bangor, Maine and in Syracuse, New York. I start to get the creeps now, because I remember the kid and me sitting in Durgin Park in the marketplace, and walking all around. I never should've been out with that kid, day or night.

My mind is jerking through thoughts like a copy machine popping out pages. Should I leave town? No way—if the kid ends up home, every cop would be looking for a runaway kidnapper. Should I stay here? No again, 'cause the cops can find me here just the same. My neck hurts really bad, and I want to get back in bed, I feel so weak and broken. Why would the kid steal all my money? Okay, maybe he just wanted to get away. How stupid I was to let the kid go without the chain overnight. It's my own fault, I see. I had to go and trust somebody to stick around my place without a lock and chain to hold him there. Now, I'll probably get pinched. In a way, it's almost like I don't care if the cops do grab me. But something just tells me to get myself acting normal, get in my Santa Claus suit and carry on my usual daily routine. I dress up and put my outfit on, figuring if I do get pinched, the cops will be less likely to gun down Santa Claus while he's collecting charity on the streets of Boston.

\*   \*   \*

Ringing my bell only hurts my neck some more, and I have to keep it a little crooked so I can at least stay out and buy some time. "Coins for the needy," I says, and this time I really mean it—and I think them people know it, too. Couple old folks stick a five in my beggar pot, lots of other folks throw quarters and dollars in. Looks like it could be a pretty good day, and the kids ain't even out of school yet. Just before dark could be the best time of all. Maybe today I'll even stay out after dark too, I think. Pick up a few extra bucks.

Then I think about getting mugged, like some poor sap Santa Claus did last year. Got himself stabbed for forty bucks he never would've kept anyhow, by a couple guys from Dorchester. But I figure it couldn't hurt to take the risk of staying out. Anyhow, I'd like to see a mugger try to cross me tonight.

Just around nightfall I go in some restaurant for supper, Santa suit and all. Lots and lots of little kids are peeking in the windows, some mothers and little kids come in and say hello, I says ho-ho-ho right back to them and wave. I'm a pretty good Santa Claus, I think. How many other Santa Clauses would eat their supper in a restaurant window so lots of little kids could see?

I have my beggar pot on the floor at my feet, empty now because I changed all my coin into bills and stuck them into my pants for safe keeping. All of a sudden up comes a lady with two little girls and a whole lot of shopping bags. One of the little girls has a candy cane, and the other one has a big piece of apple pie with vanilla ice cream melting on it and steam coming from the dish.

"These are for you, Santa Claus," the two girls say, and they put the sweets on the table in front of me.

"Thank you, thank you," I says to them, and then I give their mother a wink. "Merry Christmas, little angels." As they leave, I eat the pie and stick the candy cane in my pocket. The pie is real delicious. I never expected fringe benefits on this job.

Now, I'm starting to worry again about that crazy kid taking off. By now he must've gone home and told everything—about how I kidnapped him and tied him up, and then used a chain to lock him with, and how I shoved him that time. His old man will probably have half the cops in Boston up to my place like Marines storming Baghdad. Maybe they'll be at the apartment now, just waiting for me to come back.

I know what I'll do, I think as I get up from the table and make for the door. I'll head home in my Santa Claus suit, and if any cop cruisers are around, I'll just keep walking past and get on the next fifteen buck bus to New York out of Chinatown. Then I think, no way—what if the cops have a trap set and ain't in marked cars, what then? By that time it would be too late, and I'd be bagged for playing Santa Claus on top of it.

I go back on the street and get to ringing my bell in front of some old time chapel where there's a lot of light and a lot of people shopping around. I figure I'll be safe there. "Coins for the needy," I call and ring, and people drop money as fast as you please. The wind picks up stronger and stronger as the night goes on. Soon, my fingers feel the cold right through the gloves. My nose is chilly, and the air has a crisp taste of snow.

About a half-hour later, I go in the fourth floor men's room of Filene's and change. There's a couple people inside, so I wait till they leave before I stash the rest of my money. Then, I bag my Santa suit and make for home. I figure I made almost three hundred bucks today, a real good take. Not even another week left for that kind of money, though. It'll be a hard winter without the ransom. Now, I think I should've asked for less, and maybe he would've agreed to pay it.

*   *   *

I start to feel a little relieved when I get home and there ain't any cops at my door. I go in the apartment and it's dark and creepy like it always is when I get home at night. I put the light on in my kitchen. My neck is as bad as ever, I feel it while I'm stretching out my arms. I go in my room, take the Santa Claus suit and stash it under my bed and fish the money out of my pants, stick that in my empty dresser drawer. I go slouch down on a kitchen chair. Coffee would be great now, I think, and I get up and put on a pot.

I go in the den, put the light on. I look at that tree the kid had me put up, and all of a sudden I feel real mad. Suckered by a kid, I think. I look at the stereo on the other side of the room, and I wonder what in the world ever made me buy the thing, anyhow. I got no use for it. Then I think about all my money gone, and I feel on fire. My blood is boiling in my neck and face, and I'm about to knock the tree over and step on all the bulbs and smash them, when I hear a rap at the door.

Cops, I think, but I don't hear anybody say so. Then I hear another knock, and I ask, "Who's there?"

"Hello," somebody says in a thin, quiet voice.

Maybe it's Nora, the lady upstairs, I think. Last year she asked to borrow some room in my fridge for her Christmas preparations. So I go to the door and open it up. Who do I see but this little girl standing out there, holding on to a shopping bag and shivering. "I'm cold," she says.

"What's all this?" I ask. "Whatta you lookin' for?"

"Would you like to buy some matches, sir?" she says in a kind of English accent, and she steps right in my doorway. "I'm freezing."

I see right away she should be freezing. All she has on is this light coat that ain't even buttoned up, and a dark green velvet dress. She has this big fluffy hat comes down almost over her eyes, her hair long and uncombed, no mittens, and she has some socks that come up to her knees, one sock lower than the other.

"Where do you live?"

"I'm freezing," she says again. "Don't you have any hot water I can put my hands in? I knocked upon all the doors downstairs and nobody answered. You have hot water?"

"Well, I do, I guess. Where are you comin' from, anyhow?" I ask her.

"The store." She pushes a clump of hair away from her mouth, turns her face away, then she turns back again.

I got the creeps now. All I need is to get caught with some little girl who comes up to my place off of the street. "Where's your home?" I ask. "Whatta you lookin' for, anyhow?"

"Just a place to stay for the night," she says.

"Well, ahm—I don't know if—"

"Sure you do," the girl says. All of a sudden she takes off the big fluffy hat, and her hair comes partway off with it. I see in a second it's not a girl at all, but Gabriel in a cheap wig.

I grab hold of his arms, half crazy mad and half crazy happy. "What in hell?"

"You know what?" he says, pulling the wig off and holding it out like it's a tarantula. "I saw my picture in the paper. Two different papers, the *Globe* and the *Herald*. And I figured the people would be able to notice me right away, so I went and bought all this stuff at Morgan Memorial to hide myself in. You should see the old lady who worked there, she kept looking at the dollar bills to see if they were ones or fives, so I knew she'd never know I was me. I asked if I could use the bathroom, and I changed in there, and then I sneaked out while she was busy. I came back here around five, but you didn't come back so I had to find dinner in town."

Suddenly I think about my money. "Where's the money?"

I says, grabbing the kid hard by the front of the dress. I see it's hurting him a little.

He pulls himself away, then goes fishing through the shopping bag. He gets out his pants, his shirt and his coat, dumps them in the middle of the floor. Then he takes out his gloves with the fleece lining. On the bottom of the bag is a blue thing looks like an envelope. He pulls that out and opens it up.

"It's seven money orders," he says. "See? Six are for five hundred, and the other is for four hundred and eighty-seven dollars. You're the only one who can use them. It was easy, I got them in the convenience store."

"Well, you shouldn'ta done that. Most kids don't carry that kinda money around."

"I gave the bag to the lady, and told her I was doing it for my uncle in a wheelchair, because he didn't want to keep cash around the house."

I look at his face. Then I can't help myself, I take him by his arms and pull him close to me and pick him up and hug him. "Kid, you're crazy," I says. "You're crazy."

"You gonna take care of that coffee pot?" he asks.

"Yeah, and you get outa that fool dress right now. It don't do a thing for you."

"Oh, yes it does." He goes over to the sink and puts his hands under the hot water. "Now we can go to the movies. I mean, if you want. Nobody'll ever know I'm me."

I look at him and he's looking up at me with them big shining eyes. He's got another thought in his busy skull, and that's that. I blow out some air, kinda aggravated. "Okay, okay," I says. "You know, you're havin' a little too much fun bein' kidnapped."

"Whatta you want, better than that?" he says. He grabs a towel and wipes his hands. "Well, *Toy Story 2* is playing at the movies tonight, and it's only six bucks." He pulls three twenty dollar bills and a couple loose singles from his pockets.

"What's that money?"

"I saved eighty dollars at the last minute, just in case you didn't go to work for more. I had to use some of it for food and stuff. Here, I figured you'd need it."

"Good thinkin', kid."

"Gabriel."

"For cripes sake, Gabriel. Now get that dress offa you before you get used to it."

He takes off the coat and keeps the dress on for a while longer, stands around me while I'm putting seeds in the coffee pot. "Well what's takin' you?" I says.

"How do I do as a girl, anyhow?" he says. He sticks the wig back on and starts to dance around the kitchen. Then he does a bow, turns around and does another bow but sticks his behind way out. Then he spins around front and pulls up the dress way high and shows his underwear.

"You do awful as a girl," I says. "Now put your real clothes on."

"How come you're holding your head that way?"

"What way?"

"Crooked."

"Because I got a stiff neck and I had it since this mornin'."

"Oh." He finally starts putting on his pants and shirt.

I cover up the coffee pot and go sit down. Next thing I know he's getting his coat on, and he sits on a chair across from me. "What's that for?" I ask.

"We're gonna take a drive, aren't we?"

"It's about nine o'clock, kid—Gabriel. I'm bushed, can't you wait till tomorrow?"

"Aw but—aw, I don't care. I can wait." He stands up and takes off the coat and goes in the den. I see the lights on the

Christmas tree go on, and all of a sudden I'm glad I didn't knock it over. I hear him rustling around a couple minutes, then I hear some music start up with a squeal from the tape.

He comes out and sits across the table from me. I smell my coffee getting done, and I get up to pour some. "Get yourself some milk," I says.

"Crackers, too?"

"Sure, go ahead."

While we're sitting there munching away, we don't say two words. He just looks at me with some thinking going on behind them eyes. When he drinks, he puts his baby finger under the bottom of the glass. Then when he puts the glass back down, his finger goes out in the air like he's pointing at something with it.

"You know what I do when my dad has a stiff neck?" he says, and wipes a milk moustache off of his mouth.

"What?"

He gets up and comes to my side, stands behind me. He puts his hands on my neck, and they're cold from the milk glass. "Whatta you doin'?" I ask.

"You'll see," he says, and he starts to rub my neck. He digs in the muscles and presses around in little circles, pulls my head up a little, then rubs right where my shoulders and neck come together.

"Be careful, it's really sore." I start to get the feeling he's looking close at my head, and from the corner of my eye I catch him looking at my ear. "Somethin' wrong?"

"No—I just—you don't have hair on your ears."

"Am I supposed to?"

"I don't know. My dad shaves the top of his ears. Sometimes when he doesn't shave them for a few days, they grow hair on the top."

"Well, I'm glad I don't have to shave my ears," I says.

While he's rubbing my neck, I'm thinking about the ransom and the whole kidnapping thing. If old Mister Winthrop Booker don't come up with the ransom money, what happens? I think about the kid, and I know I ain't about to kill him or anything. I figure I'll just keep him until the old man comes up with the money.

I'll have to stick with the chain on his foot—and while he's sleeping, too. It all depends on the old man now. "Look, Gabriel," I says, "I'm gonna have to chain your foot again tonight."

"I figured you would."

"That's the way it has to be. From now on, any time I'm not here or if I'm sleepin', then you have to be chained."

He stops rubbing my neck. "Okay," he says, "if that's the way you want it. You know, I could've left and gone home and stolen all your money, too."

"That ain't it," I says. "What happens if I don't get the ransom? If you want to take off, then all you'll have to do is open the door and leave."

"So what's to keep me from yelling out the window?"

I stand up. "That's how you get in trouble," I says. "Because if I get here before the cops, and they start bangin' down the door, you and me'll be in the way of the bullets. So just think about that."

"What if you don't get back before the cops?"

"Then you get away, that's what. But until then, you have to stay on the chain." I go in the den, drag out the chain and lock it around his leg. "It don't hurt you a bit, anyhow," I says, "and it's plenty long enough to get around."

"Are we going to the movies tomorrow?" he says.

"Yeah, we are."

"Good."

"You tired?" I ask.

"I sure am. How come you didn't come home at dinner time? I was freezing in that dress, and I came up here three times and nobody was here."

"I worked late."

"I walked around and around downtown and kept going inside stores to keep warm. While I was in a bookstore, some guy kept coming over to me and asking me stuff, like what kind of books did I like, and if I was all alone. I got sort of scared, so I told him my father was in the store, and he left. After that I just stayed in crowded places. I heard some people talking about the Enchanted Village of Saint Nicholas, so I waited in line a half an hour to go through it. That was fantastic, it's all these old fashioned shops and houses decorated for Christmas, with mechanical people doing different things. Some of the houses had a second story, and you could see kids chasing each other in the windows, and one rooftop had a cat chasing a mouse around and around. Plus, I saw four different Santa Clauses."

"You did? Where?"

"Oh, everywhere—one in a store and the others on different streets, ringing bells and collecting."

"Did you give any?"

"Yeah, to the Salvation Army. I just tossed in some quarters." He gives a huge yawn, and I see his eyes are starting to sag.

"You wanna go to sleep now?"

"In a while—hey, you know something? I didn't wet the bed last night."

"I noticed," I says.

He looks at me. "Do I have to wear one of the diaper things tonight?"

"Yeah, you do—you never can tell. Why, do they bother you, too tight or somethin'?"

"No, I just feel kinda funny wearing diapers."

"You'd wear a dress in public," I says.

"Okay, okay, I'll use one."

When he's finally ready in his camouflage pajamas, I get the music down soft and we both kneel together by my bed, because the kid's bed is just them cushions and not high enough. "See if I can remember the prayer," he says. "Now I lay me down to sleep. Um-mm, I pray the Lord my soul to keep. Um-m-mm—"

"If I die," I says.

"Oh. If I should die before I wake, umm, I pray, I pray—"

"I pray the Lord my soul to take."

"I pray the Lord my soul to take," he repeats right after. Then he fixes his cushions and gets in bed. "Hey, Duncan? Can I ask you a question?"

"What?"

"I was wondering, how come people pray?"

"I dunno. To make sure they stay close to God, I guess."

"But—if you're close to God, how come you committed a crime?"

I sit down on my bed, kinda flabbergasted. "That's the million dollar question," I says. "Maybe I ain't so close to God. When my girlfriend went off and married somebody else, everything worth living for was blown away. I died that day. My lungs just suffocated, except my body kept living. I stopped praying, I hated God and hated the world. If somebody said, 'Oh what a pretty bird,' I'd say 'I wish I had a gun so I could pop off his head.' Then one day I was in the gun store and heard that Beatle's song, 'Let it Be.' I just listened to the whole thing. It was like God's hand came out of the sky and tapped me on the shoulder—'Hey, you ain't the only one who's gotta pay full price.' So maybe I ain't so close to God, maybe God's trying to be close to me. Maybe I just need to pray so I don't go over the deep end and buy that gun." I look at him and see his face all cloudy, and realize I said too much. I go to his bed and crouch over him—pull his covers up tight around his chin, then rub my hand through his hair. "Tuck in now and go to sleep, okay?"

"Good night." He turns over to sleep. I kill the light and go in the den to listen to the rest of the tape and think about getting that ransom.

# TAPE TEN

When I'm finally tucking myself into bed, Gabriel rustles around and wakes up. In a second he's up on his elbow. "Duncan?"

"What now?"

"How come you kidnapped me?"

"Why does anyone kidnap somebody? For the ransom money—I want something green for Christmas. Now get back to sleep."

"I mean, how come me instead of some other kid?"

"'Cause you happened to be right there, in case you forgot. Now don't bother me, I'm tired. Why do you always ask me personal stuff when I'm tired?"

"Just because I want to know why. You knew it was me, and you did it on purpose. That's what I mean."

"Because—I know your old man's got money, and I got this thing against hot shot politicians, anyhow."

"What do you have against them?" he asks, sitting up on his bed now with his knees bent in the air.

"For cripes sake, do I hafta tell you my life story?"

"No." He shrugs, folds his arms across his knees and rests his chin on top, still looking at me.

"All right, all right, I'll tell you. It's because my girlfriend married one, that's why. Big shot politician from another state—far away, where she went to college."

"Is that what was so serious that happened to her?"

"That's what was so serious that happened to me," I says. I lie down on my bed, hands behind my neck. "She was pregnant, that's what was so serious. She was having a baby."

"A baby? Was it from the politician guy? I thought you said they were just friends."

"I thought so, too." For a while I just lie there thinking back to when she told me about it. Then I says, "We were talkin' about getting married, not like we were engaged or anything yet, but maybe in about a year. Then the next time I saw her, she came cryin' to me that she was breaking off from me. I said how come, I thought we were supposed to be getting married. Then she said she was going to marry that hot shot college friend of hers. I asked her if she was pregnant, and she got mad and started telling me I was being a jerk. But I knew something was wrong, and I asked her again, 'Is it because you're pregnant?' Then she looked at me in this way I'll never forget, her face all white and her eyes on fire. 'All I'm going to tell you is I'm getting married,' she said."

"So, what made you think she was having a baby?"

"At first I just felt it in my heart, but then I heard a couple of guys, I think they were friends of mister hot shot, and they were talking about how his girlfriend was pregnant and was going to marry him, and they mentioned her name a couple times."

"Oh, that must've killed," Gabriel says. "But they had to get married if they were having a baby, didn't they?"

"I suppose that's one way to look at it. But if you ask me,

she just picked the politician because he had more money and more of a name."

"That's pretty rotten. When did it happen?"

"I dunno, a long time ago."

Gabriel perks up, lifts his head and squints at me. "Did you ever know if it was a boy or a girl?"

"I dunno." I breathe in real deep and let it out fast. "It was a long time ago, and far away. It's no use to even think about it now, anyhow."

"But you must do a lot of thinking about it, or else why would you go through a kidnapping and maybe even go to jail?"

"It's for the ransom money."

"Oh," he says, and he lies back down on the couch cushions. "Don't you work or anything to make money?"

"Well, yeah—I got myself a little job. I can work whenever I please, pick up tips for my work. But I don't want to keep that up forever. That's part of why you're here, so I can fill up my savings again. Nobody knows me, so I'm pretty safe. Nobody but one guy named Dick, and him I don't know but to talk to."

"Only one guy knows you in this big city?"

"Well, maybe like two or three people," I says. "It's real easy to get lost in a big city. People see me every day for years, they don't know my name. I don't care, either. I really don't mind."

"What do you do for spare time?"

"Oh, I see the shows, mostly. It's like a hobby. Then I just walk around, look over the city."

"Maybe you should find another girlfriend," he says.

"No," I says. I reach over and shut off my light. "I dunno, I been thinkin' about that. I guess when you really love some-body, losin' them ain't the kind of thing you can just fill up by findin' somebody else. You always know the second one is a substitute, and you'll never really give her a chance to be her own complete self, 'cause all the time she'll just be fillin' in for somebody else. One thing I found out, and that is, you can't make somebody love you no matter how hard you try, no matter how your heart screams for her. Otherwise, she's a prisoner. And I didn't want to make her a prisoner," I says, feeling my chest tighten inside.

"But—what if some lady really likes you, but you don't know it because you never let yourself find out? That wouldn't be fair either, would it?"

"Lots of girls liked me, but I didn't like them back. I tell you, it has to work both ways, no matter what way you look at it."

"I know, I know, but what I mean is, you don't know if it might work both ways if you don't at least give it a try."

"I guess what it really is," I says, "is because I'm just scared of it happening again, and then where would I be?"

"So where are you now?" he asks.

I can't say anything to that, so I just says, "Shut up, kid, okay? Just go to sleep."

I hear the chain clink as he gets himself all buried in his blankets and settles down. It's quiet for a long time, and finally I says, "I dunno. Maybe you're right. Maybe I should find another woman." But I don't know if he's even awake to hear me.

Then a second later, he calls me again in the dark.

"What now?"

"Remember the other day when I got up and I didn't wet the bed?"

"Yeah, I remember."

"Well, that's the first time I ever remember not wetting the bed."

"Is that so—the first time in your life?"

"Yup. I just wanted you to know that."

"When you wet the bed at home, ahm, what do your mom and dad think?"

"They don't care too much. Well, that's not really true. My mother tries not to let it bother her too much, but my father really hates it. They've taken me to about ten doctors, and all they said was I'll outgrow it. We tried all kinds of things, like not drinking anything after seven, and setting the alarm to get up in the middle of the night, and making me change my own sheets. Then last year my dad started saying stuff like, 'I don't know where you get this habit, nobody in my family ever had this problem.' "

"Don't sound like such a bad problem to me," I says. "I knew a few kids who wet the bed."

"Well, none of my friends do. You remember I told you about my friend, Justin? Well, one night he stayed over at my house, and of course I wet the bed like always. Then my father came in the room and said something like, 'Can't you even control it when your friend stays over? My God, the whole neighborhood's got to know it, now.' Only Justin never told anybody and never made fun of me. He invited me to stay over at his house a few times, but my parents would never let me because of it. Oh, I don't care."

"You always say, 'I don't care,' but I think that's when you care the most."

"If you really want to know, that's primarily why I ran away from home."

"Sounds like you ran away because your old man kinda makes fun of you."

"No, not really. Well, I guess he does—sometimes. You want to know something really, totally private? One time my mom was away for a couple of days to help her sister, 'cause she just had a baby, and my dad made me stay in my wet night-clothes for a whole day."

"He did? Didn't you ever tell your mom?"

"No, he told her. He was totally having a rupture about me

and started blaming her for it, and she got twice as mad and yelled right back at him and said she didn't see how abusing me was going to help anything."

"When did this happen?"

"I don't know, last summer, I guess."

"Oh," I says. "What about now—you miss your mom and dad?"

"You want to know the truth?"

"What else?"

"Well, right now I don't miss them. Sometimes I do, and I want to go straight home, especially when I think about how awful my mother must feel. But then I think about how you went out and got all those things for me like clothes and food. And got the Christmas tree and all the things to put on it, and let me help decorate it. And how you taught me some prayers so I won't be scared sometimes. So right now I sort of miss them, but not a really lot."

"So if I just bundled up all your stuff right now and drove you home, would you be happy?"

He don't say anything for a while. Then he says, "What about the ransom money?"

"Well, I don't mean I'm gonna do it, I just mean how would you feel?"

"Pretty good, I guess."

"How about your friends, you miss them?"

"Yeah, and they're going to be wicked jealous. I just hope I'm home in time for Christmas."

"Well," I says, "I think I better get some sleep."

"Me, too. Can you put the light on for just a second? I want to go to the bathroom, see if I can wake up dry tomorrow."

# TAPE ELEVEN

Tuesday morning I'm up before the kid, getting some eggs made for breakfast. I have a plan to get some kind of a fire under that Mister Winthrop Booker. It'll have to wait until dark, I think as I put on some toast. All of a sudden the kid tears into the kitchen and clanks the chain to the bathroom. "I didn't wet it!" he calls from behind the door.

"Good," I says. Almost got me a heart attack.

"You going to work today?" he says on his way out.

"Yeah, you stay here and watch the TV."

"Oh, television's boring in the day. You only have eight stations, and all they have is money shows and soap operas."

"So whatta you want to do?"

"Anything, as long it's not the television."

"I'll go and buy you a couple things from the store, books or somethin'."

"How about a couple of comics, or something I can make? Oh, I know—how about a puzzle?"

As soon as I eat, I head out and buy the kid a few things to keep busy with for the day. He's so excited he don't know where to start. While he's looking through everything in the bag, I go in my room and snake out my Santa suit from under the bed, then head for the door. I'll be back for supper," I says, and I go out.

"See you, thanks," he calls after me.

Before I go down town, I stop off in the savings bank with my money orders. I tell them I want to open up an account, and they get all hyper and send me to a desk to sit down. I wait ten minutes and a nicely dressed lady comes and sits down with a pile of papers. Sign this, sign that, and I never seen the beat of all the signing I have to do. I just do what she says, and she looks at my money orders and leaves the desk with them. Then about five more minutes later she's back with them. Right about now I'm thinking I could've been out there collecting all this time. I check my Santa suit bag to make sure everything's there.

"Did you want to deposit the entire amount?" she asks.

"What? Oh, sure, the whole thing." And she gives them to me to sign on the back, then tells me to wait again. Another ten minutes, and she comes with a little green card, has me sign that, and then she goes and runs it through the computer.

Finally she gives me a receipt and says, "Thank you. You should get your ATM card in the mail within a few days. Just be careful not to lose it."

"I'll be careful, all right." I stick the receipt in my wallet and figure I'll keep it there all the time.

*     *     *

I really like the idea of playing Santa Claus. I guess it's because I have such a good outfit, and lots of people come just to see me on my corner. Around lunchtime, I'm almost ready to take a break when I see Dick Murphy walking up in the crowd. "Hey, Mister Murphy!" I call.

"Hey, Santa Claus," he says and comes up and shakes my hand. "You must keep yourself in great shape ringing that bell." He squeezes my arm.

"Hey, Dick, I was wonderin'," I says. I look around to make sure there ain't too many people close by. "Are you gonna be busy on Friday afternoon, Christmas Eve?"

"Friday?—I'm hoping to get off work a little early, then I have a party that night, that's all. Why?"

"Well, it's nothin' too important. We can talk about it tomorrow night."

"Oh—right. See you at the Lantern."

"Don't forget now. Tomorrow night."

He hustles away with a smile, giving me a thumbs up sign. Murph is always in a hurry, it seems. He just comes and then is gone in no time. I get right back to my ho-hoing for about fifteen minutes before I remember I'm overdue for lunch.

\* \* \*

At suppertime I close up my corner and head off for the department store dressing room. I take off my Santa suit and bag it, then I stash the money in my pants. Passing through the toy department, I see hundreds of things piled sky high, and I feel like I wouldn't know where to start if I was ever a kid nowadays. There's people swarming through everything, grabbing this and that, packing up carriages like there was no tomorrow. I look around, see a few toys I think the kid might like to have. Maybe I can get him a bunch, since he don't like TV in the daytime. I grab a cart and fill it up with some big things and some little things, plus my Santa suit bag.

I have to wait in a long line to pay, and when I get there the guy zips through all my carriage in a minute flat. "Comes to seventy-eight dollars, ninety cents," he tells me.

Suddenly I remember where my money is. "Ahm—can you hang on a second, I hafta get my money."

"Whatever," he says.

"Can you please hurry?" Some lady behind me can't wait.

I run to the dressing room quick and take out my money bag, pull myself together, and run back to the guy at the counter. "Here you go, there's a lotta change." I lay out forty-six dollars in bills, then I start counting change.

Can you check me out first, all I have is four little things," the lady says. "You people should have special lines for people who don't do this Christmas Hanukkah thing. Really!"

"Just cool your jets," I says to her. By and by I get sixty-two dollars paid off, and I see I'm down to a pile of nickels and dimes. I see the line is getting longer behind me, and the other counters have huge lines at them, too. In a minute I'm down to nothing, and I only have sixty-six bucks and nine cents paid. "That's all I got," I says. "I come in every day—can I pay you the rest tomorrow?"

"No, I can't do that. Sorry, but you'll have to return something."

"You're a real pal." I take out two toys that add up to about twenty bucks and hand them over. "Here."

"Thank you," the guy says as he punches in the new numbers and gives me my change.

"Thanks a lot," the lady behind me says.

"Oh, can you give me an extra bag, my old one's fallin' apart here," I says, showing him.

The guy's got all my stuff bagged now, and he don't even look at me. He just gets another bag and flings it over the counter at me and goes back to his work.

On my way home, I figure I don't want to give the kid the toys right yet. Best to save them for Christmas, in case his old man don't pay the ransom and he ends up having to stay. That way he can at least feel like he's having some kind of Christmas. I go to my Dart and open the trunk, toss them in. Then I go in my apartment and see this contraption with about ten birds hanging from the light in my kitchen. "Hey Gabriel," I says. "Where'd that thing come from?"

He comes out of the den holding this electronic gadget in front of his mouth. "What? Oh, the mobile," he says, sounding like a robot. "That's what you gave me today. It took three hours to make, do you like it?"

I reach for the gadget and he hands it to me, then I put it over my own mouth. "Yes, Earth boy, it is a magnificent display." I hand it back to him and he presses a button on the side, and suddenly it starts bleeping and blooping. "Did I buy you that thing? I didn't even know what it was."

"It's pretty neat, Duncan. I like it, thanks. What's that you bought?" he asks.

"This? It ain't anything, just some work clothes. Did you eat lunch?"

"Yup."

"Get your coat on, we're gonna go out for supper," I says. I go in my room and grab some money, and put my Santa bag under the bed. Then I unlock Gabriel from the chain.

"Not my coat," he says. He runs in the den and starts to change real fast. Soon he comes out wearing the green dress. "Today, I'm going to wear my own socks under the girl socks. I almost froze yesterday." He sits down on the kitchen floor and puts the rest of his clothes on, then he grabs the wig and puts that on, too, and fluffs it out over his shoulders.

We head out, and he pulls the fur hat on for a final touch. I see he'll need some mittens, so we pass by a store that sells only kid clothes, and we go in and buy some knit mittens there after he makes sure they're the right color to blend with the coat.

"Call me Hannah Montana," he says.

"The hell I will."

Kid's dying for Chinese food, because they got a lot of vegetable type stuff, but the only one we see is a takeout place. We settle for a cafeteria and get macaroni and cheese, only I get a piece of chicken for myself as well.

Outside, he gets full of his after supper craziness. He tears up and down the street like a pup. Then he runs around me in a couple of circles and takes off again fifty miles an hour, looking too much like a boy for that dress to do much good. When he comes back he asks what movie we're gonna see, will it be *Toy Story Two*? I says, "Yeah, why not," and we go. Soon as we get in our seats, he turns to me with a worried look.

"How can I go in the men's room with a dress on?"

"You don't, smart guy," I whisper real soft to make sure nobody can hear us. "Just go in the ladies' room."

"I never went in one before."

"Oh, for cripes sake, just go."

He stands up, then sits again. "I'll hold it in," he says.

About ten minutes later the movie's going and has half the place laughing already. All of a sudden Gabriel stands up and scrambles over me. "I'll be right back," he says and takes off down the empty half of our row. In a while I see him walking up and down the aisle, looking for me. I stand up a little so he can see me. "Did you find the ladies' room?" I whisper when he's sitting again.

"I just used the handicap one, it's unisex."

\*   \*   \*

At bedtime, Gabriel asks me if I'll play some music. "Sure," I says as I chain his ankle. I'm goin' out tonight, so if you wake up and I ain't here, don't worry." He don't answer, and I see his eyes are closed already. I leave the music on a while longer till I know he's sleeping.

I get a city map open on the kitchen table and check my plans, even though I know my way by heart. Then I quietly get some money from my dresser, put on my coat and head for the Dart. It takes me about ten minutes to get the old rust bucket started up. Then I turn on the radio and go.

Half-hour later I'm driving down their street. I see the house, a big white one with no lights on the bushes or candles in the windows like some others. That's good, I think. It'll be harder to see me. I drive past it, park the car way out of sight on a side road, and walk back. I see the new Jaguar in the driveway, and check to see if there's any motion detector lights around, and I don't see any. Now, I sneak up to the back of the garage and check the doorknob. It's unlocked. Real slowly I turn it, pushing the door open just enough to squeeze myself inside. My heart is pounding in my chest and neck so hard I can hear the throb in my ears. No alarms, no nothing. There's another truck type thing in the garage, a dark green Ford Expedition. On the other side of that is the door to the inside of the house, and it's covered with metal and has two steps going up to it. I get myself over to the steps and sit down on the bottom one. Somehow, I ain't even afraid of getting caught, it's almost like something outside me is making me do this.

From inside I hear muffled sounds of talk, but I don't quite get what the words are. I lean my ear closer to the bottom of the door. I think it's him talking.

"Come on, now, why don't you come to sleep. We've done everything we can today."

"I can't sleep. I can't keep my eyes open, but I'm afraid to close them," I hear her say through the ringing in my ears. "How did this happen? How can anybody do this to my beautiful boy? Oh, my God, what if they're hurting him?" I hear her crying now, and it sounds as if he's trying to comfort her, but I can't quite get what he's saying. Then his voice gets a little louder, and I hear him plain as day. "I don't know whether to take this seriously or not. I mean, he had that knapsack all packed with stuff he wears day after day, and his Game Boy with extra batteries?"

"But he didn't take them. He didn't take them." Now she's crying right out loud. "Whoever did this better watch out, because I'll kill them, so help me, I will! Oh, Win, who could have done this? Can't you think of anybody?"

"I'm trying to tell you, he could have done it himself. I have to admit I've been a little hard on him at times. He has run away before, and this knapsack was packed for a reason."

"He wanted to go on the Polar sleepover, can't you see that? He wanted to go so badly, he probably packed for it."

"Three weeks early?"

"Oh, come on—like father, like son."

"God, I'm completely baffled. I'm wiped out. Why would he leave his schoolbooks home? Why would he not take the school bus? If he's kidnapped, I can only think it's by some psycho son of a bitch, and my blood runs cold just to think of it. Feel my hands, they're freezing. What's the thermostat on in here, anyway?"

"I don't know, I didn't touch it. I'm cold, too."

"I just—my mind is fried. I don't know what to do here. I know we have to show the knapsack to the investigators, that's a start. Maybe they'll have some insight that we can't see right now. But other than that, I'm flat out. My ear hurts from being on the phone all day and night, and my eyes are blurring. I'm going to bed."

"I'll be along in a minute. I'm going to take some Pepto Bismol—I don't ever want to live through another night like last night."

I hear a sound like somebody going up some stairs, and then I hear water running. After a while everything is dead still, and I get on my feet. My left leg is asleep and I have to shake it hard to wake it up. Step by step I head back around the Expedition to the door, and duck out even slower than I came in.

In the driveway I prowl up on the Jaguar real easy with a key from my pocket. I go around to each tire and let all the air out, right down to the ground, and even though it's taking a real long time, I just keep at it while my heart keeps beating harder and harder in my throat.

When it's done, I sneak away and make it back to my car, pretty glad I used gloves tonight. Then I think, what happens if they can trace my footprints in the snow? I get fidgety about that, so I decide to buy a new pair of shoes. I drive to a K-mart and buy a pair real fast, then on my way home I dump the old ones off of the Cambridge bridge into the Charles River. I seen too many movies to get caught with a stupid thing like that, and it don't cost hardly anything to get a new pair of shoes.

# TAPE TWELVE

At home again, I get undressed for bed and tuck myself in. I don't feel like sleeping right yet, my head is still busy. Little by little I get the feeling I did something wrong. Then I get it—I should've never let the air out of those tires. They'll know I was there, and they'll be crawling all over the place for hair samples and footprints and everything. They'll figure I'm in the area, and that gives them more pieces of the puzzle than they should have right now.

On the floor I see one of them comic books I got for the kid, and I pick it up. I read the whole thing, page after page, but not really paying attention. Then I lie down to see if I can catch a wink. I roll over, try to stop thinking.

Pretty soon I'm thinking all over again, so I get out of bed. Maybe something like some tea or some cocoa will get me to sleep, I think, so I find a box of cocoa and take out some milk and put a pan on the stove to heat. While I wait, I sit at the table and rest my head on my hand.

By and by I look at the kid, and he's sleeping sound as ever.

The light from the kitchen goes in the room a little, and he turns over to get it off of his face.

I put some cocoa in a cup, then test the milk, which ain't hot enough. I stand there and wait, stirring the milk and staring into it. My mind wanders, and I think of how I'd probably have my own kid now, maybe two. I don't know what makes me think of it, but I get a sudden picture in my head of that first time I met April Ferris at the Towne Diner. I was pretty new and they had me on mornings, and one day the manager called me up and asked if I could come in and help close for the day. It was my day off, but the regular worker was sick, and there would only be one person left to do everything, so I said okay.

I went in and got my apron and grill hat, and when I walked out to the serving area there she was, kneeling on the floor behind the service counter, putting all the pieces of the milkshake machine on a tray to carry them to the kitchen. I remember it like it was just this afternoon. I couldn't believe my luck, to meet somebody so pretty and easy to get along with. We became friends right then. Soon our schedules changed, so we were working together three days a week. I had a girlfriend and she had a boyfriend, but over the next few months we found ourselves both single again, and we dated each other a lot, mostly going to movies and for pizza afterwards. And did we talk, more in that one year than all the talking I've done since then. That was the best year of my life. I was so sure every year from then on would be just as good, and even better. Dick Murphy and I had a bunch of guy friends that used to come in as regulars, and I remember being jealous over April—nothing to fight about or anything, because they never asked her out. It was just they were single guys and friendly with her.

And I remember the first time I kissed her. One night we were watching TV, and she fell asleep on my lap. I touched her cheek with one finger and pushed some of her hair aside so I could see her ear. I think my heart was pounding loud enough for her to hear it. I watched her and studied her, and realized how much I wanted to see her face like that every morning of my life, so bright and fresh and pretty. And I remember thinking even if we both got old and got lines in our faces, it would be like lines from a map of roads we went down together. That was when I put my face down and kissed her on the cheek. She woke up a little, and she turned her face so we could kiss each other, and we kissed like bashful school kids. Then she went back to sleep. I remember even the way she breathed, how it came so softly, and the sweet smell of it, and how she curled up because she hated to feel cold, and the way a vein on the side of her neck throbbed with every beat of her heart, and how she sometimes moved her lips in her sleep like she was just about to speak.

I remember when things started to fall apart, even though I never saw it at the time. I told her I was planning to go to college myself, and all through the summer before she went on campus, she kept showing me these catalogues. But then when fall came, I never signed up. That got her pretty disappointed, and we had a kind of fight, like I said something about being afraid I wouldn't do well. "You know, you're afraid of a lot of things," she said. "You're afraid of success, that's what. Because then you'd have to grow up, and be responsible, and maybe start speaking correct English instead of some blue-collar dialect." I never thought I would want to hit a woman, but that time I really wanted to hit her. Not that I would do it. But now I look back and realize I only wanted to hit her because she was telling the truth, and I didn't want to hear it.

Funny thing—after that I kept feeling the sting of what she said, and so I applied to Northeastern for the Law Enforcement course. I went back to my high school and got a couple of my old teachers to write letters for me, and somehow I got on the waiting list for the spring trimester. I never said anything to her about it, because I wanted to have an acceptance letter first. Sure enough, I got in at the last minute. I bought my books and everything, and then I was going to surprise her that day.

But I never got the chance. When she told me she was leaving and was going to marry her hotshot college boyfriend, you could've mowed me down with a Mack truck, all eighteen wheels, and I would've never felt a thing. It was a February day, not too cold, and I was wearing this sweater my mother knit that April loved on me. So there she was, shivering like I never remembered her shivering before. I went to put my arm around her and she pulled away and said, "Duncan, we have to talk." I took off the sweater and told her to put it on, and she did, and it came down to her fingertips and over her bottom. And she told me all about how she was going to get married, and we kind of argued over it, and I remember saying to her, "Isn't there anything we can do?" And she started to cry and said, "I'm so sorry. It's just—I think it's just best if we don't see each other anymore."

I couldn't think of anything to say, so I just said, "Did you ever know that I love you, April?" But that was like somebody who gets a knife in the heart saying, "What'd you do that for?" It was a question you'd never hear the answer to. We both stood there for an infinite minute staring at each other, mute, story over. She might as well have been on Pluto—there wasn't as much as a shimmer of warmth left in her eyes for me. So, I left her standing there crying, and I drifted away and never saw her again. I guess she still has the sweater, though. The college books I bought—I don't even remember what became of them.

The milk is starting to steam and roll together as I stir it. Now, I think about Gabriel and how he'll be gone as soon as this kidnapping thing is over. I don't like to think about that much. It only makes me tight at the throat to be reminded of what I don't have, like I been robbed and shoved out on a dead-end street. Not that I much want to get back on the main street. After all, living the way I been for this long ain't hurt anybody else, and it ain't hurt me either. Well, the Santa Claus thing might be kind of a lie, but at least people give me cash because they want to, it ain't like taxes.

I taste the milk and it's piping, so I pour some in my cup and stir it. Next thing I know, the kid's awake. I hear the chain jiggling a little, then I see he's up and going for the table. He sits down across from my seat at his usual place.

"Hey, Duncan, whatcha got?"

"Just cocoa."

"Can I have some?"

I look at him, and I'm almost ready to tell him to get back in bed, but I grab another cup and spill some of mine in it. Then I put some more milk on the stove. "What'sa matter, Gabriel—can't you sleep?"

"No. Lots of times I wake up in the middle of the night. Then I can't get back to sleep for a long time, because I get scared."

"Whatcha scared about? There ain't nothin' to be a-scared of here."

"I dunno, just things." He runs in the den and then comes back out with a candy cane from the Christmas tree. He unwraps it and stirs his cocoa with it, then sips. "Mmm-mm, just hot enough so it doesn't burn," he says.

"Well, what kinda things?"

He shrugs his shoulders, looks in his cup. Then he looks at me again. "I dunno, things like being dead or something."

"Well," I says, "it is kinda scary to think about. But you won't die till God wants you. And when he wants you, he'll make it okay for you."

He don't say two words more, he just keeps on sipping his

cocoa and sucking on the candy cane, and eyeing me now and then. By and by the rest of the milk is ready and I mix up more cocoa and pour it out.

"You feel better now, kid?"

"A little."

"Okay. You go back to sleep. I'm gonna go out for a walk."

Gabriel rubs his eyes and goes back to bed dragging the clinking chain with him. "Good night, Duncan. Thanks for the cocoa."

*     *     *

Boston at night is a whole different kind of world than what it's like in the daytime. Most of the streets are empty, you can see the steam coming up from the gutters and stuff. The buildings seem higher in the dark, and the cold feels even colder when there ain't a whole lot of people shopping around. I keep on walking, figure I'll head for the Zone tonight because it ain't too far.

I see they got a lot of cop cars prowling around. The folks in Chinatown are trying to shut down the Zone because it's at the edge of their neighborhood. Couple weeks ago somebody stabbed two college boys real bad, one of them died the other day in the hospital. I'm always afraid of getting mugged, so sometimes I keep about twenty bucks in a wallet and the rest of my money in my shoe when I walk around here. That way if them hooker pickpockets come by, I'll have something enough for them to steal so I don't get my throat sliced.

I keep thinking about them flat tires, and about what happens if I have to go back to Mister Booker's house again. I just hope this ransom deal works. I go to the Common, check out the bushes near the horse statue like I done a couple times before. It's an easy spot for the ransom to get delivered—public place, lots of escape routes. My plan looks better all the time.

Back in the Zone, I make for one of the Triple-X-rated shows, the two o'clock showing. I see about a dozen other guys in there, and two got women with them. Halfway through the show I get bored. You can only watch so much of somebody else having sex. Plus, my new shoes are starting to make my feet feel tired.

On my way out, something crazy happens. I'm walking down Washington Street and I see this young girl, must be about fifteen or so. She's leaning on a lamp post smoking a cigarette. Her glossy black leather pants are skimpy and only come down to her shins, and she has these pointy high heels that are so big, I could see almost an inch of empty shoe at the backs. She has a big coat on, comes down to her knees, but it's open and her tiny waist is showing with this ring through her belly button—and she's shaking from the cold, anyhow. When I go past her, she throws the cigarette in front of me. I stop and look at her face. "Whatta you doin' out here, kid?" I ask.

"Give ya good time for a twenty dallah bill," she says in a kind of Southern accent.

I point my finger right to her face. "Listen here—no kid talks like that to me. Where's your home? What are you, stupid? Girl like you could get hurt out here."

"Get cash, too," she says, and she grins a chuckleheaded grin to me. I see her eyes are all puffy and red. She smells funny, like smoke and sweat and perfume. I start to think about taking her, because she's offering and I wonder what it might be like with somebody so young.

"Twenty dallah bill, mistuh."

"Listen, you—you makin' it so rich out here, how come you smell like a subway? How come you wear them size fifty shoes?"

She don't say a word, just looks at me with her bloodshot eyes, and plays with a gold chain she has around her neck.

"What'sa matter with your own house, kid? How old are you, anyhow?" I says.

"Eighteen. So lay off my case, Mistuh Clean." She takes out another cigarette and turns away.

"Yah, and I'm the Archbishop o' Boston. Why don't you get on home, kid?" I says. I take her wrist and feel how awful bony it is, and the skin is dry and creepy, and I know I wouldn't take her now even if she was naked in my room. "You want twenty bucks, I'll give it to you, but you get on home."

She starts giggling right at me, and next thing I know she takes my wallet out of her pocket and flashes it back and forth at me. "Don't worry, mistuh—you already give me your money!"

"Hey! For cripes sake, you're a thief on top of bein' a tramp." I snatch the wallet right back from her, and she's still giggling. I take twenty dollars out and give it to her, and she sticks it in her pocket and starts to shuffle on away in them oversize heels. I turn and start back for home, and while I'm walking I can still hear her shoes go clop, clop down the street. What some people will do for money.

\* \* \*

It's good to get home, I think as I go in the door on the first floor landing and climb up the three flights of hollow stairs. Hallway always smells like detergent, the maintenance guy keeps a pretty clean place. It reminds me of when I was a kid, when we used to drive to Boston to visit my Italian grandmother in the North End. The summer air would be thick with the smell from bakeries and the sounds of the saints' feasts, and I'd open the big door and go in that cool hallway and smell that detergent smell that I know as sure as I know sky blue. Inside my apartment is warm, and the Christmas tree smell makes me feel good as I undress for bed the second time in the same night.

I go in the bathroom and wash my hands with hot water for a long time, take off the smell of that poor crazy girl out there. I'm always afraid I'll catch something like a disease. Shame that any kid would even know where the Combat Zone is, but I guess that ain't ever gonna be helped no matter how many cops they got running around. Then I think, maybe even some cops visit them poor slobs.

I get done washing, then I shut the lights and go in my room and get in bed. That hot cocoa must've knocked Gabriel right out. I feel plenty tired myself, finally.

# TAPE THIRTEEN

Next thing I know, I'm awake and it's light. I look at the clock, see it's about ten after ten—it's Wednesday already. Gabriel's still sound asleep. I get up and get in my clothes, and before he even wakes up, I throw my coat on and head out. I drive to a phone booth at a shopping center.

"Mister Winthrop Booker?" I ask.

"Yes, speaking."

"Did you get my message?"

There's blank silence for a long while.

"You still there?"

"Oh, my God," he says. "Yes, I did get your message, and I'm not happy about it. Look, I don't know who you are, but—"

"Look you, Mister Winthrop Booker. Your kid's in a lotta danger now. It's a hundred thousand bucks in a brown paper bag. Now listen to this good. You get that dropped off in the bushes near the horse statue in the Boston Common."

"Where?"

"In the bushes by the horse statue in the Boston Common. A brown bag, and remember good what I tell you. If it ain't

113

there by three o'clock Friday, your kid starts to suffer. If it ain't there by three-thirty, you don't see your kid again."

"Look, I can get the money. I can get it."

"Good."

"But for your sake, I should tell you one thing," he says to me. "This isn't going to work, pal. Why don't you just put the boy in a taxi and send him home? No questions asked. Think about it."

"Hey!—Alive or what?"

"It isn't going to work, pal."

"Well, you got more to lose if it don't. Get that money there, and if somethin' goes wrong, it's your regret."

"It's not going to work," he says again.

"Well, goddammit, he's your kid!" I says, and I slam the phone down.

\*    \*    \*

The kid seems to know I'm in a horrible mood when I get back from talking to his father. When I go in the bathroom I see his pajamas hanging up to dry on the bath towel rack. "Wet the bed again, huhn?" I ask.

He goes in the den with his head down, takes a bulb off of the tree and sticks it in another spot, fixes some tinsel, then goes and sits down on the couch without the cushions.

"You keep yourself pretty clean, kid. That's good."

"Something wrong, Duncan?"

"Yeah, plenty is wrong. Whatta you doin' over there, anyhow?"

"I have a loose tooth."

"It's bleedin' all over your hand."

"So what, that always happens when I pull on a loose tooth."

Suddenly I hit on an idea. I go to the medicine chest and take out some cotton. "Hey Gabriel," I says. "Put this cotton around your fingers when you're pullin' on the tooth."

"How come?"

"Well—it'll help hold the tooth. Now lemme go, before there ain't any people left shoppin'." I fetch my outfit, taking it under my arm. "Hey, Gabriel."

"What?"

"How'd you get your clothes changed without gettin' the chain off?"

"I don't know. I took it all off my left leg first, then—oh hell, you believe everything. I just went looking for the key. I wasn't about to wait for you so I could change, you know. I was going to leave it off, but I thought you'd get mad."

"You thought right, kid. Now go wash your mouth, and then do what you please till I get back."

\*   \*   \*

I never seen the beat of all the money I get today. Old ladies with bulging shopping bags in both arms, old men tightening scarves against the cold, all kinds of business people and bums, guys and girls walking together, looking all romantic—they all say "Merry Christmas," and with a smile they toss a couple coins or a dollar bill in my pot. Everything's going pretty well until from behind me I hear a young woman's voice say in a tight scared tone, "What're you doing? What? Huh?"

I look around in the crowd. I see some big moose of a guy holding a girl against the store with his body. She looks confused. I see the guy's making like he wants to hug her or something, but I see his midget partner working a hundred miles an hour in her handbag. The midget pulls out a fat wallet and shoves it in his coat, closes up her bag. That's all in a second, and by this time I see it's the art girl. She's just about to scream out, but the big guy turns and disappears into the crowd again.

"Hey, hey!" I yell out. "Those guys just stole your wallet!" I drop my bell on top of my beggar pot and start to run after the midget. I see there ain't any cops right around, so I grab him myself and tell him to give up the girl's wallet. The art girl is standing there crying mad, and everybody's looking at her as she tries her best to get composed.

The midget's looking at me like I'm crazy, and then the other guy, mister moose, bumps me from the side. I see he's got a knife in his hand. He says to me, "What's it gonna be, walk or ambulance? Get lost."

I don't know myself too good when I'm scared. My arm shoots up and knocks the knife out of his hand. Then I hit him a shot in the chest.

People are gathering around. Some guy comes up and grabs the midget from behind to hold him. A cop on horseback is coming now, and the big crook picks up his knife and escapes fast around the corner, blending away with the crowd.

The midget guy is still standing there.

"Gimme the wallet and I won't turn you in," I says, and the midget takes out the wallet and gives it to me. Then he pulls free from the guy holding him and runs down the street to catch up with his partner.

I hurry back to the art girl and give her the wallet.

"Thank you—thank you," she says. She looks at me for a second and then grabs my hand, then sort of pulls away like she's a little shy. "That was very nice of you." She's breathing ragged still, like she's tired. She's awful pretty, her eyes and hair are glossy brown and she has a couple freckles I never noticed before, only now she don't have all the braids like she had last week. Her face is still a little white, probably from people standing around making like it's a TV show.

I says, "Don't worry, it was nothin'. Why should they get your money?"

"That's the second time that's happened to me," she says. "They work so fast, those pickpockets. People usually turn away, or they just don't realize what's happening."

"I don't turn away," I says. "I was almost gonna be a cop at one time."

"Really?"

"Yeah." Calm as I can, I pick up my bell and start ringing again. She's still standing there.

"Hey, do you always play Santa Claus? I mean, you're not Santa all year round, are you?"

I see she's trying to lighten up some, so I says, "Of course I am. Why, don't I look it?"

"Sure do. You're one of the few Santas I've seen that looks so real. A little skinny, but…"

"Thanks," I says. I'm getting a little fidgety—I don't like her spending all this talk on me—makes me too easy to notice. "Don't you have a name?"

"Santa Claus."

She laughs, has a kind of laugh like Gabriel has—full and tickled, friendly. It makes me want to take another look. She's the first girl held my hand in a long time.

"No, come on," she says. "I'd believe it if I were still a kid."

"Okay, okay. I'm really Duncan Wagner."

Just then, a guy with two cameras comes up to me and says, "Say buddy! I got a picture of you taking the woman's wallet back from those losers. Good deal, I work for the *Herald*—could I get your name?"

"Ahm—I don't really want that printed," I says.

"It's possible we won't have room for it," he says. "Just a formality, that's all. What's the name?"

"Okay," I says. "Joseph Elmer."

Now the news guy gets nosy. He asks, "What charity do you work for?"

"Well," I says, "I work for the Children's Charity of Boston. It's a little organization, private, you know?"

"Very good," says the guy. He takes it all down and says, "Thank you," sticks a dollar in my pot and takes off.

The girl is still standing there. "Hey, I thought you said your name was Duncan Wagner."

"It is," I says. "I don't like to get in the papers. I like my private life."

She smiles and her eyes twinkle. "Santa Claus with a private life."

I see she likes to talk with me. This time I'm not in a down mood. The stuff about the wallet and the knife and the photographer, and making up a lie to cover myself all worked out so good, I figure I'll play along.

"Don't you ever get out of that costume, though? What do you do the rest of the year?"

"Odd jobs," I says.

"Oh. You know, I'd like to meet you at a better time. Really, I would like to."

"Well, uhm." I was thinking of telling her I'm engaged, but then I figure that would be a fool thing to do. She's telling me right out she wants to meet me. I got burned before and I know I won't let it happen again, but at least I could talk to her over a coffee some time.

"Oh, I see," she says. "You're involved with someone?"

"Ahm—not really. No. But after Christmas—"

She looks a little confused, like she don't know what to make of what I'm saying. But I'm thinking about Gabriel and the kidnapping. Up till right now I had nothing to lose if the kidnapping went sour. With this girl in front of me, it's like I'm married to my kidnapping plan. I see I buried my freedom to go out with any girl for the whole time I'm with Gabriel. "Well," I says, "I'd be glad to meet you, but I think it'll hafta wait till after Christmas. Why don't you give me your number and stuff, and I'll call you some time—you alone?"

She turns, looking over her shoulder, then turns back to me real fast. "Oh, you mean—ahm. You'll have to call me and see," she says with a fresh smile that comes up with a dimple I didn't see before. She eyes me and blinks while she's writing.

"What's your name, anyhow?" I ask.

"Martina." She shows it written out. "My friends call me Tina."

"Oh. That's pretty." I ring my bell, look at her and give a smile because she seems so happy I saved her wallet. She gives me the piece of paper and I put it in my wallet with my savings bank receipt.

"I have to go," she says, and she puts her hand to my white glove and holds on for a second. "Thanks again."

"No sweat," I says. "And if anybody else tries that funny stuff, just bash his nose with the bottom of your hand, like this." I show her with my hand on my nose.

"I hope I never have to," she says, waving as she walks backwards. "Bye!"

\*   \*   \*

Time to quit work, and I'm still feeling better than I felt in more than ten years. I hurry up and change in the department store, then shove off for home loaded with cash. For a second I have this thought about scrapping the whole plan and sending Gabriel home, and picking up a phone to call Martina. But then the idea goes away, almost like it burns right out, and it don't come back.

In the apartment, the kid already has the lights twinkling away on the tree, and has the stereo piping some Christmas music. I sneak in my room and stick my Santa suit under my bed. Then, I think, I better find a new place for it, the kid's nosy and may try looking in the bag when he don't have anything to do one time. I go to my closet, stick the bag on the shelf. Then I get a bag in the kitchen and put some old pants in it, plus an old shirt. That one I stick under the bed.

All this time the kid's in the den putting a puzzle together. He's so busy with it he don't even follow me, he just says, "Hi Duncan," kinda absentmindedly.

I take the key to the chain and unlock him, tell him to hurry up and put on that foolish dress. "I made extra money today. We're goin' out to eat."

"Oh, fantastic!" He jumps to his feet and starts to change right in front of me. After he's done, he sticks his hand to his mouth and works on the loose tooth. "I tried to get it out again today, but it doesn't want to come out."

"Lemme see it," I says. I look in, then I touch it to see how it's coming along.

"See how loose?" he tries to say while I got my finger in the way.

"That ain't so loose," I says. "Look, let's go to town because I'm gettin' hungry. When we come back I'll help you take it out. Get your coat."

He puts on the girl coat and the wig, then he runs in the bathroom to try to comb the wig a little. "Can you put the hat on me?" he says. I fit the hat on him as he pulls the mittens out of the coat pockets, and we hurry out the door.

# TAPE FOURTEEN

After a good supper at a pub down the Theater District, we go out in the cold for a walk. The wind is brisk, has a clear bite to it. We stop in just about every store we pass, and Gabriel checks out all the toys and the sports stuff, the skis and skateboards and the newest electronic gizmos. In a big department store he stops before a mirror and looks at himself, then lifts his leg up and fixes his stocking, folding the top down nice and neat. "I think my lips are getting chapped," he says. He goes to the cosmetics department and picks up a lip balm stick. "We have to buy this." He pops the top off and puts some on his lips, and it smells like cherry bubble gum.

In the toy department, Gabriel grabs my coat all of a sudden. I look at him, and he's trying to hide behind me. He turns around and starts walking the other way kinda fast, so I follow him. Then he ducks down another aisle, and as I turn down behind him, I hear some kid say, "I could swear that girl looked exactly like Gabriel Booker."

We hustle down the doll aisle, and as we go, some guy calls over to the boys and says, "Come on, Ken. We're late. Let's go."

Gabriel does pretty good, he just keeps walking until we get to an exit, and we shove on outside. When we get a way around the corner, he stops in front of a closed bank window. "Those were two kids I know from school," he says. "They recognized me, I know they did. I could tell by the way Kenny looked at me." He puts his hands on his chest. "My heart is pounding. What if they tell?"

"I dunno. I don't think they could say nothin', because they don't know for sure. They'd hafta know, don't you think?"

"They see me every day, though. What if they tell Kenny's dad and he calls the police?"

"I dunno. Even if they did, we'd be long gone by the time they start looking."

"I wonder what they'd think if they ever found out it was me."

"They'll never know, so just forget it. Let's get outa here."

"Maybe some day I'll tell them."

"Never mind that—you could get in big trouble."

"But it would be a good story, don't you think?"

"No. Because you wouldn't want your friends to know you were ever in a dress."

As we walk among the people shopping, Gabriel bends down to hold his knees now and then. "Whatta you doin'?"

"My knees are so freezing. Let's go in another store."

We're right at the corner crosswalk with about fifty people waiting for the cop to let us across. Just as we start, moving like sheep in a herd with our heads down to fight the cold, a big blast of wind comes by. Right in front of the cop, Gabriel's hat blows off. The wig shifts over and he claps his hand down on it. Cop looks straight at him, keeps staring as I run to get the hat.

I plant the hat on him again quickly, and we blend back in with the crowd on the sidewalk. I turn my head to eye the cop, see if he's still watching, and he is. I see he takes out his radio and starts talking on it. Cops are always talking on their radios, but this time there's reason for me to have the willies.

We duck in another store to warm up and make plans. We're in the store about five minutes when I see a different cop come in the door. "Hey," I says real softly, "here's what you're gonna do right now. I want you to take this money and get right down the subway as fast as you can. Ask the person in the booth how to get to Haymarket, and go there on the next train. Wait there for me, anybody tries anything funny, just go hang around some lady with an umbrella or somethin', she'll help you."

"What are you going to do?"

"Split up, that's what. Now get movin', hurry up. If a cop follows, just run."

"I can't beat a cop," he whispers all worried, and he looks over to where the cop is standing by the cash register lady, giving her small talk.

"You won't hafta, I'm saying just in case. Now go."

For a while I move around the aisles, see this display of cookie dough that makes round cookies with a green Christmas tree in the middle. I grab one and stop off at the cash register right next to the cop, and ask for a pack of gum, just so I can act normal. Once outside, I hear the rumble of the train underground. I'm heading for the stairs to the station, but I don't go down them just yet. I wait at the side, where some guy is selling papers, and look back to the store I just left. That cop comes walking out the door, and it seems he's trailing me because he starts to walk my way. So, I hurry down the subway stairs.

For five minutes I wait, feeling more and more frazzled until a train finally comes by, and I get on. I see the cop never followed me down here, so I try to relax. When I get to

Haymarket, I hop out fast and look for Gabriel along the plat-
form. Down the far end past the closed up news stand, I see
him sitting on a bench with a paper opened up around him. It
covers his whole top, and it looks like a girl's legs dangling off
of the bench. There's a lot of other folks at the station, so I
don't make a scene. I just walk up real slow to the bench and
sit down next to him.

"Want some of the newspaper?" he asks with a big grin.
His eyes are all bright.

"Yeah, gimme some."

"That was a pretty good plan, you know, Duncan. It
worked perfectly. How did you think of it so fast?"

"Oh, I'm pretty good at gettin' away from dangerous things,"
I says.

"You know—do you mind if I say something personal?"

"It's nothin' new with you."

"Well, I was just going to say that you don't look like a doc-
tor or a professor or anything, but you're sure pretty smart."

"I'm so smart I get headaches," I says. "Now lookit what I
found in that store."

"What is it?"

"It's a big salami of cookie dough. So let's get home, I have
things to do tonight."

"Will it take long?"

"No, about ten minutes."

"Good, because I've had to go to the bathroom for almost
an hour now. Let's hurry."

*     *     *

Seems like every night we have cocoa before Gabriel goes to bed.
Tonight he's sitting at the table in his pajamas waiting for the
cookies to be done, jiggling his leg up and down and clanking

the chain. He's got his candy cane already unwrapped to dip. "Hey Duncan," he says. "Do you think I'll really be able to go home in time for Christmas?"

"I dunno. I have a plan that'll help, but I can't be sure."

"What is it?"

"Well, I thought up the perfect ransom note."

"Tell me."

"That you'll hafta find out after you go home," I says. I fix the cocoa and put the cups on the table. The kid mumbles something and I look at him. He's got the fingers in his mouth, yanking at the tooth.

"What's that you said?"

He takes his fingers out. "I said, will you help me pull this tooth? It gets in the way of my tongue."

"Drink your cocoa first."

"Okay." He swizzles his candy cane in his cup, then tastes the cocoa. It burns his mouth, and he spits the sip back in the cup, wags his hand over his mouth. He gets up and clinks across the kitchen to the den and puts on some music, then gets the milk out of the fridge, dumps it upside down in his cup. Only a couple drops come out, hardly enough to cool his cocoa.

"I gotta do some shoppin', don't I?"

"Yeah, some crackers and some good stuff like Ring Dings and Little Debbie star crunch and things like that, plus milk and some more peanut butter."

By and by the cookies are done. The whole kitchen smells like a bakery store. When I put a dish of the cookies on the table, he scoffs about a half a dozen.

When we're done with our warm up, I get a fresh chunk of cotton. "Okay, gimme your mouth," I says. I look in and see the loose tooth, shaking it a little. Around the gum it bleeds, and the blood follows that little crack between the gums and the teeth all the way around his mouth. "Get your tongue outa my way." I grab the tooth between my finger and thumb and give it a yank.

The kid's eyes spring up with tears, but he doesn't make a peep. I show him the tooth on the cotton. He sticks his tongue in the space of the pulled tooth and it gets all bloody. Then he looks at me and smiles.

I pack a chunk of cotton in the space until it's real wet with blood. "Now go and get your mouth washed out with ice cold water till that blood stops," I says. While he does that, I put the cotton in the little jar with the other bloody pieces. I cover the jar and stick it in my pocket, and set the tooth on the table.

After a while he comes out of the bathroom. "What's that you're doing?" he says.

"I'm writin' a ransom note, that's what."

"How come you're wearing gloves?"

"You tell me, smart guy."

"Oh—fingerprints. Hey Duncan, I want to show you something. Look at my teeth, see up top where the eye tooth was missing? It's starting to grow in—see that little white thing showing? My mom says it takes long for them to come all the way in."

"Pretty good, pretty good. Now don't bother me, I hafta get this done."

"Where's the tooth?"

"Right there."

"Good." He picks it up and looks at it, then puts it back down. "It's a perfect tooth, no cavities."

"Do you mind if I keep it?" I ask.

"Sure, take it. That's for you to remember me by."

"Thanks. Are you ready to sleep now?"

"It's only eight-thirty."

"Well, go turn on the TV, then."

He watches TV for a while as I finish up the ransom note. I get the little jar with the bloody cotton from my pocket, pick up the tooth real careful with my glove on and drop it in the bottom of the jar. Then I cover the jar and stick it back in my pocket. When I go in the den, I see the kid is dropping off to sleep. He keeps shaking himself awake. I take him into my room and put him in his bed, skip prayers tonight. After all, I'm in too much of a hurry for my nine o'clock appointment.

# TAPE FIFTEEN

My watch says five after nine when I walk in the Blue Lantern past a few customers standing outside for a smoke. Looking around, I don't see Dick Murphy. There's a strong smell of pizza and beer. Suddenly from behind me, two hands grab my shoulders. I spin out of the grip and see it's old Murph laughing away. "Hey, Murph—how you been?"

"Great, Duncan, just great. What's it been, ten years? God, we're getting old."

"Nah, you look okay," I says. We pull off our coats and find a booth. A dumpy waitress wearing too much makeup puts the pizza menu on our table and takes our order for a pitcher of beer. I ain't much of a drinker, but I sure feel like having a couple tonight. "Yeah, it's been a while," I says. "Right now, I'm busy with my work, playin' Santa Claus and all."

"That's a hell of a job, huhn? When I first saw you, it took a while to figure it out, 'cause the Santa suit was prime stuff—how'd you get that job?"

"Ahm—" I lean over the table and look at Murph. "Children's Charity of Boston. It's a small group."

"You pocket any of it?" he smiles, the blue eyes gleaming with a touch of deviltry.

"Who, me? Oh—every last dime."

He busts out laughing, slaps the table top. "Hey, let's get a plain pizza," he says, and folds both menus closed. "Tell me, Duncan. How've you been getting along? You ever marry that girl you were going with back then—April, wasn't it?"

I look out over the noisy room. "No. Never did."

Murph crosses his hands over his chest and shuts his eyes. "Oh, how can you mend a broken hea-eart," he sings, just like the BeeGees. Then the waitress comes over with our pitcher and two mugs. She laughs a little to see him singing, but I don't. It's like, the same thing that makes me like Dick Murphy, that big and loose way he talks and acts, is now rubbing salt on me. I see he don't mean it or anything, but it's happening. I try to block it out. Murph stops singing and turns to her. "One large cheese pizza," he says, then pours both our beers to overflowing.

"Here's to the good old days," he says. "They sucked, but here's to 'em anyway, and to Christmas, and the future."

"You bet, pal!" I says, and we clink glasses and drink.

"Hey Duncan," Dick says with a lowered voice. He leans over the top of the table. "Remember the other day you told me something about Christmas Eve? You said it's important. What's cooking?"

"Oh," I says. "Are you gonna be around Friday at three, three-thirty?"

"Sure," he says.

"Would you do me a little favor?"

He turns his hands palm side up, raises his eyebrows. "Shoot."

"It ain't much," I says, almost whispering. "You know where the horse statue is down on the Common?"

"Yeah."

"There's a bunch of bushes there. We Santas have a special place where we put the cash when we get full. Then at the end of the day it goes to the bank."

"You leave it out in the bushes like that? I never would've thought."

"Well," I says, all of a sudden feeling like he can see right through my talk. No matter how much I thought of the ransom and how it should be delivered, it always came down to an open, public place. But now that I'm telling Dick about the Santa collections in the bushes, it sounds bogus, and I know he's either going to accept it or not—that's the gamble. "The other guys say they used somebody's trunk in the Boston Common garage last year, but they had two robberies. I dunno, puttin' it in the bushes seems pretty lame to me. Who am I to say? They tell me so far there's been no problem."

"So, you want to trust me to bring your cash there?"

"No, I want you to pick up the day's take. I'm in charge of gettin' it to the bank. I volunteered for Christmas Eve 'cause the other guys have families—but I won't have time to go get it myself. I'll still be in that Santa Claus suit, and I'd be a sure hit for a muggin'."

"Then you'd get your mug in the papers!" Murph laughs out, then guzzles the last half of his beer down, refills it and tops mine off, too. "Geez, you ain't in much of a good mood tonight, are you Duncan?"

"I'm all right."

"Okay. Well, it sounds like a pretty simple favor."

"Whoa, that's great—" I says, and I'm trying to keep myself calm even when my lungs are trying to huff and puff. "Come at about three o'clock. Go to my corner first, to make sure I'm there and ready. Oh—and there's somethin' in it for you."

Murph looks at me and squints an eye. "A surprise from Santa Claus?"

"Oh, you might say that."

Both of us bust out laughing, and people at tables near us turn and look. So, Murph waves at them. Then some get huffy, but most smile.

"You serious?" Murph asks.

"Sure I am."

He shrugs. "I won't complain if you don't."

Our pizza comes bubbling hot, and we both dig in. I feel a lot better now I know Dick will make the pickup for me. For the next half-hour we gab and eat, though I go easy after two beers to keep my mind clear. When the waitress brings the check, Dick grabs it and says, "It's on me, Duncan—for Christmas."

"Aw, you don't have to," I says, but he holds up his hand. "Okay, Murph. I'll get it next time."

"Okay, let's go."

"What're you up to for the rest of the night?" I ask.

"Well, Eileen'll be coming back about eleven. Till then, I'll just sit home, relax. Why?"

"Nothin'—just wonderin'."

"You want to come over and meet Eileen? Come on, we'd be glad to have you."

"No—really, that's okay—another time. I gotta get some milk and stuff at the Sunny Corner, and I got a few other things to do."

"Okay. Hey, it's great to see you're still kicking, Duncan. See you Friday."

*   *   *

I knew what I wanted to use the kid's tooth for as soon as I saw him tugging and yanking at it. There ain't a better ransom note in the world than a part of the kid's body with some blood. I remember one time some kidnappers cut a guy's ear off and mailed it to his home. Anybody in the world can tell it's a kid's tooth with an awful lot of blood like it was pulled. And it's the truth—I'm the one who yanked it, and I made sure I kept the jar without fingerprints.

I drive my old Dart over the same roads I used before to get to Winthrop Booker's house, only this time I start to wonder if this might not be a good idea. He might have cops around to guard it since I let the air out of the tires. Damn, now I wish I didn't do that. Plus, I don't know if I really need to deliver the tooth to get the money. But something tells me to do it anyhow, almost like even if there's cops and I get bagged, so what?

I park a good block away from their street, and with my gloves on I give the tooth jar another wipe with a clean rag. Then I walk down the street like anybody else would. Everything is normal, and nobody is on the street but me as a car drives past and turns a corner up ahead. Going near the Booker house, I stay in the shadows of the bushes. Suddenly, my ears perk up when I hear a garage door open. I pull in close to a big bush and wait. My heart is in my throat, because I hear two men's voices talking from the side of the house.

"Look, I can't tell you what to do. It's a shitty situation."

"What happens if they don't return Gabriel? What happens then, Eugene?"

"Win, come on. Here, let's just get the car inside."

I hear the car doors open and close. While they're starting the engine, I creep up the front stairs and stick the jar in the letter box. Then I slip in the note. Real careful I go back down the stairs to the bushes. Just as soon as I hear the garage door close, I start back to my car. I see there's no trouble about footprints getting traced, because the sidewalks are shoveled clean, and I made sure not to step in any snow. But I drive away in a hurry all the same. They could find that note anytime—all somebody has to do is go to the door and see the letter box is stuck open with that jar.

\*   \*   \*

The late news wrap-up is on when I get home, and I sit down to watch. Looks like the whole nation is interested in the kidnapping. One professor from a big college says that there's been a lot of kidnapping attempts around Boston this year, and the disappearance of a girl in Newton this fall may be connected to the Booker kidnapping. He says the kidnapping and murder of a local boy last summer still has many area people enraged, and so what happened today in Somerville is understandable. Then some guy comes on, says he's a crusader for capital punishment. He says kidnapping is one crime that should be punished by the death penalty.

Now they have a replay about what all the talk is about. Just this afternoon some guy from Somerville got attacked in a mall parking lot by about thirty people. Seems he was with his nephew, a kid some people thought looked like Gabriel Booker. Some witnesses said the boy was yelling at the man, "Just take me home, I want to go home." Next thing the guy knew, he got jumped by all these people and beaten and kicked until he was nothing but a bloody mess on the ground. He's in the hospital now, and they have nine people under arrest, and they're looking for more on security videotapes.

For a while I get the creeps, knowing I'm the reason this guy got trampled. I never figured this thing would get so out of hand, or that I would have all those people against me. I ain't some kinda Timmy McVeigh. If they knew I'm being pretty square with Gabriel, they wouldn't carry on so. But I guess I can't make them know either, or else I'd never get anywhere with the ransom deal.

Then I think more about them clowns on the TV, saying all that bunk about kidnapping. I never knew about any girl in Newton disappearing, so how could that make me kidnap Gabriel? And what happens when some mother or father takes their own kid like in a lot of divorces? Then what are they gonna do, give them the gas pipe?

I get tired of watching by and by, so I get ready for bed.

# TAPE SIXTEEN

Thursday morning I wake up and look at Gabriel. I see he's awake over there on his couch cushions, but he don't start gabbing right off like he usually does. "Hey, Duncan?" he says.

I look closer at him, see his eyes are kinda watery. "What'sa matter? You been cryin'—homesick or somethin'?"

"No," he says. "I think I'm sick. I think I might have pneumonia. I got it when I was little and I had to go to the hospital for a week."

He sounds like hell, his voice is all raspy and whiney. His face is white and his eyes look like that young girl's eyes I saw down the zone. I get out of my bed and go in the bathroom, get the kid a glass of water and a Tylenol. "Take this now," I says. "I'll go to the drugstore and get some kid medicine later on."

"I'm scared, Duncan. What if I got pneumonia?"

"Do you feel the same as when you had it?"

"I don't remember. You know you can die from pneumonia."

"Don't worry," I says. "You just got the flu or somethin'. Now go back to sleep and stay in bed until you feel like gettin' up."

"You know what?"

"What."

"I didn't wet the bed last night, that's one good thing." He pushes away his covers and clanks off to the bathroom, then clanks back in his bed and curls up in a ball with the blankets tucked around him. I see him shiver a little, so I take the two blankets off of my bed and put them on top of him. "Thanks," he says, and shuts his eyes.

In a while he's asleep again—easier for me to get stuff done now that the kid ain't under my feet. I get shaved, then dress up for an icy day. I grab my Santa outfit and head for my morning collections.

Out on the street my brain starts to addle up on me. I can't seem to think straight, just too much stuff is going in one side and out the other. I feel awful fidgety. Suddenly, I remember the jar with the tooth and the bloodied cotton inside. My head starts to clear up. Now, I see it's the newspapers I need, to find out where to go from here. I look in my beggar pot and see I already have about twenty dollars' worth of coins and bills, all collected in about an hour.

A couple teenage girls come along, hang around to talk. I says, "Ho-ho-ho, what is it that Santa Claus can get you for Christmas?"

The girls giggle a little, and one throws a quarter in and pulls on the other one's arm. The other one pulls her arm free, and stands in front of me. "That's the best Santa Claus suit I ever saw," she says, and then turns to go.

"Hey," I call, "Will you do me a favor? I need a newspaper."

They turn back to me, and I give one of them money from my pocket. They both run across to the news stand and buy it. When they come back, they hand me the paper and take off.

Bottom of the first page has a little clip, "Kidnapper Terrorizes Family." It says, "The kidnapper or kidnappers of

Gabriel Booker have allegedly left the tooth of the child with some pieces of blood-soaked cotton in the mailbox of the Booker home. Preliminary comparison with dental records shows that the tooth in fact belonged to Gabriel Booker, according to the family dentist who was called late last night. The blood-soaked cotton was sent to a laboratory for analysis, along with a hand-written ransom note." Then it went on to say, "So far no individual or group has claimed responsibility for the abduction. State Representative Booker initially refused to cooperate with ransom demands. However, he is prepared to consider the demands, provided he gets some guarantee the child will be returned safely home." Wow, I think. Now that's news.

The paper also has more on the guy from Somerville who got beaten up. They say it's a miracle he has no broken bones, and he's expected to be sent home some time today.

By lunchtime I have about a hundred dollars. Since I have a lot to do today, I pack up my Santa stuff and go home. Gabriel is sitting in the kitchen in his pajamas with a soup dish in front of him. He looks pale still, his head resting on his hand. He looks up at me and says kinda weak, "Hi Duncan." Then he looks back in the soup dish.

I go in my room and stash my Santa suit in the closet, then come out and see there's a little pan on the stove, and next to that is an empty can of Campbell's chunky vegetable soup. "You cooked yourself some soup?" I ask.

"No, the good fairy made it," he says.

"Oh shoot, I forgot your pills."

"It's okay," he says. "I already took one of the ones you have. I don't take kid medicine, anyhow."

"Okay, okay." I go to him and put my hand on his forehead like my mother used to do when she thought I was too sick to go to school. The kid's awful hot. "Hey," I says, "why don't you go back and lie down, get some more sleep. I want you to be all better when you go home."

"Okay…hey, Duncan, are you going back out again this afternoon?"

"Yeah, I have a lotta business to take care of."

"Can't you stay awhile?"

"For what?"

"I don't like being alone."

"Aw, come on. Just lie down and sleep, and then you won't even care if nobody's around. Go on, and I'll put one of them tapes on."

He lies down as I put some music on, then after he's conked out, I put my Santa money in my drawer. Now it's peaceful, and I go in the kitchen to figure things out. The paper says old Winthrop Booker is ready to pay up, which is good news. The bad thing is that I have to wait until tomorrow and see if it's the truth. But I'm all prepared if it ain't the truth and the money ain't delivered. I decide I'm gonna make a couple fire cocktails to throw at the old man's house, that's what I'll do. I ain't taking no for an answer this time, I'm through taking no for an answer all my life.

Before I go out, I grab the kid's robot voice toy. My car takes a good long while to start, coughing and wheezing like an old dog. While I wait for it to warm up, I try a few buttons on the robot thing. I can't really understand my words on the springy button, but I like the other button that makes my voice sound like Darth Vader. By and by I'm ready to roll—I can tell when the heat comes on. Once I get to the highway, I look for a phone booth and find one on the side of a gas station.

"Mister Winthrop Booker?" I ask through the voice toy.

"This is his wife, no, he's not in at the moment."

I feel my heart stop right in the middle of my chest. "Well, this is the bad guy," I says with my finger pressed hard on the button. I hear her gasp. "I just called to tell you good news. Your son is guaranteed home safe and sound if the ransom is delivered on time tomorrow afternoon." I hang up before she has a chance to say a word.

I get in my car and drive over to the pumps, then open up my trunk. Real carefully, I fill up an empty plastic jug and screw the cover on, then finish filling my tank. The smell of gas helps me stop thinking about how fast my heart is beating. Next, I head off to a drugstore to buy some cotton for wicks, and this time I don't forget the kid's medicine. I stick his voice toy in the bag so I won't forget that, either.

Back home, I take the plastic jug down to the cellar. I feel my hand wet and see the damn jug has a pinhole leak. It's only in the handle, though, not bad enough to change jugs. The cellar is musty smelling, and the cobwebs on the beams shake down dust when I walk past them toward the shelves. I leave the jug on the floor, reach up to the shelves and find six bottles to take upstairs for washing.

I try to keep quiet at the sink, so the kid won't wake up. When I'm at the last bottle, I hear the chain clink, and there he is. He squints his eyes and moves up close to watch me, puts his hands almost on the cotton box. "What are the bottles for?" he asks.

"Hey, I got your pills," I says, and I reach in the bag behind the voice toy and give him the little bottle. "It's been a few hours so far, so you might as well take one."

"What are the bottles for?" he asks again, looking at me with his eyes full of impatience.

"Ahm—I was just makin' some Christmas decorations. You know, how you put candles in the tops of the bottles?"

"Yeah," he says, and he goes in the bathroom and I hear him fill up a glass with water. He comes out, stops again, and says, "But the tops are too big for candles, and I don't believe you, anyhow." He puts the medicine bottle on the counter, lifting up his foot to rub near the chain, then goes back to bed.

"Hey—hey Gabriel," I says, and I go in and sit on my bed. "I'm gonna use them for making some noise around your old man's house if he don't come up with the ransom."

"What kind of noise?"

"Just to throw the bottles, that's all."

"How come you got the cotton?"

"I got that because I like to have it around. I used a lot when I pulled out your tooth, remember?"

He looks at me with them big eyes all cloudy. "I still don't believe you," he says. "How come I smell gasoline, huhn—how come?"

"I just put some in my car."

"Yeah, I bet you're going to try to set my house on fire for real, like you said you would. I thought you were only saying that, Duncan. I didn't think you really would." He looks down at his feet and I get up off of my bed and crouch down next to his couch cushions, putting my hand on his hot face.

"Get that gas smelly thing away from me. I don't like you, and I hope they catch you and put you in jail."

I stand up. He turns over in bed away from me, and pulls a blanket up to his shoulders. He covers his head with his arm. Now I feel myself blazing inside.

I go to the kitchen and grab a bottle and throw it hard against the stove. It just bounces, so I pick it up again and whip it harder. It breaks all over the place. Then I grab another one and bash it, and then another. The place is full of a horrible racket. The next thing I know, Gabriel is behind me.

"What are you doing? What are you doing?" he says. I whip around and see he's crying, real scared.

"Whatta you think I'm doing, stupid?" I says, and I shove

him back away from me. He stands there looking at me with his mouth open, and the tears are just falling down his face.

He runs in my room and goes in my drawer, takes out the key to the chain and unlocks it from his leg. I grab him, but he squirms out of my way fast and bolts out and down the stairs. I'm after him in a flash. He's zooming down the steps and around the corner, and I'm almost up to him when he trips and smacks his knee against the wall. Then he goes tumbling down the last stairs right into the big front door.

My heart is in my throat as I stand over him. He's lying against the door, looking pretty hurt. I only hope he didn't hit his head on those stairs he fell down. I pick him up easy, and now most of the mad is gone out of me. As I carry him back up, I see his knee is skinned and his new camouflage pajamas are torn there.

I elbow my door shut quickly, and thank God there weren't any people coming in while I was chasing Gabriel. I carry him to my bed and make sure he's all right, and I can tell he is because when I ask him something, he just turns his head the other way and pouts and folds his arms. "Hey, Gabriel, I ain't gonna do anything stupid. You should know that by now. You should know."

"Why did you say you were going to burn my house down?" he asks.

"I just said it to scare your dad, so he would pay."

"How come you were getting the bottles ready, then?"

"Ahm—they were just gonna be smoke bombs, to scare your old man. That's all." I pick up the chain from the floor, see the key inside the lock. I take the key out and get ready to chain his leg again, but then I just drop the chain on the floor and put the key in my pocket. "You should let me clean up that cut and put a Bandaid on it."

"Look at my pajamas—a big rip." He spreads the material open and his knee comes through. While I clean his scrape, he looks at me with a frown. "Did you call my dad today? he asks.

"Yeah, I called. I said you'd be returned safe if they pay."

"How did he know it was you?"

"It was your mom. She answered the phone, and I told her to give your old man the message."

"Well, how is she supposed to know if it was really you or just some crank calling up?"

"I dunno. I'll just call again and make sure they know it ain't a joke."

"How will you do that?"

"Never mind, I'll do it," I says as I take the broom out and sweep up all the glass from the broken bottles.

*   *   *

Around supper time the kid stumbles up off his couch cushions and comes to the kitchen doorway. "My stomach feels funny," he says. Before I can even think, he starts to throw up. It ain't like those little pukes you see in the movies either, but a real spill, all over the floor. I grab a kitchen towel and give it to him, and he goes to wipe his mouth with it, but then throws up some more. In just twenty seconds my kitchen's a mess and he's slumped back down on the couch cushions, hiccupping. "I'm sorry, Duncan. I didn't know that was going to happen."

"It's okay, it's okay," I says, and I grab my big spaghetti pot and give it to him. "Just use this if it happens again." I can't think of how to clean it up, so I just get a sponge and the dustpan and keep cleaning until it's all done. Then I wash my hands a couple times and go check on him. He's lying on the couch cushions looking very small, and I feel low and miserable, because there's nothing I can do. I got no appetite to make supper now, so I just make the kid cups of boiled water to sip, so his stomach will settle.

I have him sleep on my bed now, 'cause it's more comfortable and stays pretty warm—better than any couch cushions could do. I figure I can sleep on the cushions anyhow, it won't do me no big harm.

Later on while I'm watching TV, Gabriel comes in the den and sits on the couch next to me. "Hey, Duncan," he says. "I feel a little better now."

"Good. You want more hot water?"

"No, that's okay."

For a half an hour we sit together looking at the TV and the tree lights. He don't say a word and neither do I. Suddenly there's a knock on the door, and we both look at each other wide-eyed. "Stay here," I whisper, and I get up and go to the door. "Hello?"

"It's me, Nora from upstairs."

"Oh, hello—hello and Merry Christmas." I open up the door and Nora is standing there with a plate full of cookies.

"I wanted to give you these, I just baked them today."

"Thank you so much, that's very nice of you."

"Listen, I heard some noise in the corridor today, like something fell?"

"Oh—yes, that was me! I'm sorry about that. I dropped some groceries, they fell down the stairs."

"It sounded like somebody fell. You didn't get hurt, did you?"

"No, no. I'm all in one piece."

"Okay, as long as I know what it was. I get so worried, you hear about break-ins all the time."

"Yes, I know," I says. "But everything's okay."

"Now listen, I'm going to go stay with my daughter and the kids for a few days. They'll be coming to get me tomorrow morning."

"Okay, Nora. I'll keep a lookout while you're gone. Those kids are very lucky to have you for a grandmother."

"Thanks a million," she says.

"And thanks for the cookies—they remind me of my mother." I wave to her and close the door, grabbing myself a cookie. I take the plate into the den and go over to Gabriel, pat him on the head.

He gets up and turns off the TV. "Hey, Duncan?"

"What?"

He gets down on the floor and pulls a tray out from under the couch, with the puzzle half done on it. He stays down on the floor and starts to fiddle with the pieces. "Will you help me put the rest of the puzzle together?"

"Now? But you're sick, you have to rest so—"

"I've been sleeping all day."

I see there ain't going to be any changing his mind. So, I sit on the floor with him and we work together and talk like old friends that knew each other all our lives. After a good while on the puzzle, I sit back a little and just watch him. His face shows he's really interested. Must be about a thousand pieces to that puzzle, but he fits them together like I make a peanut butter sandwich with crackers. By and by he catches me staring and he looks up. He just smiles, then goes back to his work.

Times like now I wish I was married, wish I had a kid just like him. All my old hurts come up, the worst hurts in my life, hurts that made me wish to die or disappear in a big city. It's a high price to pay for kidnapping him, now that I can see just what I'm missing out on. I wonder what life will be like after he goes home for good.

"Hey, Duncan?" he looks up. "You didn't call my dad. You better call him and let him know it was really you."

"Don't worry. I'll call."

"I'm going to sleep now. Maybe we can finish the puzzle tomorrow. We have to, Duncan—it's our last day."

I look at him. "Don't count on it yet."

"How come?"

"You think your old man will come up with the money?"

"If he says he will—I know he'll get it if he says he will." On his way to the bedroom, he stops in the kitchen and goes to my Saint Joseph statue. He picks it up and looks at it. "How come you have this?" he says, and he hands it to me.

"This used to be my grandmother's. It was given to me when she died. Saint Joseph is like the most underrated saint. People use him to sell their house, and they don't even care about him being the foster father of Jesus."

"Sell their house?"

"Sure, it all goes back to when Joseph was a carpenter. He was old for those days, like thirty. In his town were a bunch of beautiful teenage girls, and one of them was Mary. And Joseph did some carpentry work for Mary's father, Joachim. Mary really had a crush for Joseph, 'cause he was handsome and strong, and he teased her and made her laugh. She was only sixteen or so, and she used to hang around a lot when Joseph was working. She liked the way his beard curled near his chin—see how they did it on the statue here? Then Mary discovered she was pregnant, and her parents were gonna send her far away so she wouldn't shame her family. Nobody knew who the father was, and Mary swore she never slept with a man. So Joseph said he was gonna marry Mary, even though the baby was not from him. Once they were married, they had to go to Bethlehem and report for a census and taxes."

"I know that story, I saw it on *A Charlie Brown Christmas*," he says. "Mary was just about to have the baby, and Joseph kept looking and looking for a place to stay, and the best they could find was a barn behind an inn."

"That's exactly right. Joseph found a home for Mary and Jesus. And after Jesus was born, Joseph brought him up just like he was his own son, and taught him to be strong and kind. After that, nobody knows what happened to Joseph. He just faded into history." I put the statue back down on the counter. "Except now, people just bury him in the garden to help them sell their house."

"Really? How come? That's not very nice to put Saint Joseph in the dirt."

"I dunno. If you think about it, they should pray to him to help find a home, not sell one—or to be a good father… Or maybe even just to be a husband."

Gabriel goes in the room and gets ready to lie down on the couch cushions, and I hold him back.

"Sleep on my bed tonight," I says, "and I'll sleep on the cushions. You need to get better." He climbs in bed, and I pile on the blankets and tuck him in. He reaches up and puts his arms around my neck for a hug, and at first I start to pull away, but then I see him looking up at me. I put my arms around him and hug him. On my way out I shut the light. I kick the chain on the floor and stop a second, then I just walk over it, leaving it there.

\*     \*     \*

Later on I drive to Bickford's with the space toy and go for their outside phone. This time Winthrop Booker himself answers. "Just in case you wonder," I says, "it was me who called your wife earlier today. I guarantee that your boy will be returned safe and sound if I get the money delivered on time— tomorrow afternoon, at three."

"How do I know?" he says, kinda worried.

"Because, it's your kid's lower left tooth, and there's four pieces in the cotton bunch. Your kid likes to talk a lot, too. And if you want him—"

"Okay, so that's all in the papers, pal."

"Mister Booker."

"Yes."

"Do you shave your ears?"

"Excuse me?"

"I said, Do—You—Shave—Your—Ears?"

There's silence for a while. Then he says, "All right, all right. The money will be there."

"That's good," I says, and hang right up.

I'd love to go in Bickford's for some food, but I know I better not even think of it. If old Booker traces the call, I could be bagged in a matter of minutes. Instead, I get in my car and drive off a few miles till I find a small restaurant, and I go inside and take a booth, grab a newspaper. It's the same edition I had earlier, only I didn't take the chance to read much of it.

I look again at the article that says, "Kidnapper Terrorizes Family," and then I turn the page. What do I see but that picture of me in the Santa Claus suit! My heart jolts in me, and wouldn't you know it that the waitress just happens to come by at that moment and ask what I want.

"Just a roast turkey platter and some salad would be good," I says. Then I look back at the paper. I can't get over how huge that moose was that I smacked in the chest, and he's only in the background running away. The midget is all blurry, but I'm pretty clear. Under the picture it says, "Daring rescue made by street corner Santa Claus, Joseph Elmer. Elmer recovered a woman's wallet when alleged assailant (right) cornered her and alleged partner (foreground) was caught in the act of picking her handbag. Police are warning shoppers to be especially cautious during the holiday season."

Soon my food comes and I can't believe how hungry I am. Then I remember I never ate any supper. The turkey is just what I need. Least I don't have the kid gawking at me like I was doing something unusual, just having a piece of meat. While I eat, I read the funnies.

Snow starts to fall real heavy on my way home. The ground is getting covered right before my eyes. In town the roads are slippery and my bald tires aren't much for handling. By luck I don't run into anything, and I get home grateful.

Tomorrow is Christmas Eve, and the ransom should be paid. That means tomorrow night I should be able to get Gabriel home. How to do that is something I never thought about. Maybe I'll drive him to a corner near where I picked him up, and have him walk the rest of the way. But then, wouldn't the news hounds love it if he showed up at home in a stretch limo.

Too many things could go sour on me tomorrow, like if Dick Murphy don't show up, or if the cops trail him and take him down, or if I get found out, or if something happens to Gabriel. It's going to be a risky day from the start, and with the snow on the ground it'll be even more trouble to stand on a corner all afternoon and freeze. But I'm committed, so I have to get through it.

As I'm getting ready for bed, I remember I didn't have the kid say any of his prayers. I set the couch cushions together, then turn the middle one over because of the stain. After I'm in my covers on the cushions, I get up again. I lift the covers off of the kid and check to make sure he has on his night liner. He does—I could tell by the bumpy outline under the pajamas. He moves a little, then turns over in his sleep. I put the covers back on him and then get settled on the cushions. Then I say two prayers tonight, one for me and one for Gabriel.

# TAPE SEVENTEEN

I sleep lousy. All night long I toss and roll, finding my covers on the floor and the couch cushions separated, with my knee in one crack and my backbone in another crack, touching the cold floor. I have to pull it all together again and try to sleep, but my head keeps me from it. I feel like something is buzzing all through my veins.

I figure by this time I should be used to living like this, what with the kid being here a week and all. It ain't like that, though. New things keep coming up, and all I keep thinking about is getting caught. Like, what if there was a piece of my fingerprint on the kid's tooth? Or what if the cops recorded the phone calls at Winthrop Booker's house? So far it's been too easy, and I keep wondering if I should've thought things out more.

And the kid is another thing. He starts out running away from home and ends up kidnapped. Then he runs away from being kidnapped and ends up coming back again. I stole him from his family and tied him up, chained him up and roughed him up, and now we're better friends than most my friends ever been. Partly, I'd like to get back to my old self and have my own routine. But partly, I want to have him around, even keep him for myself. He's good company, and I like him because he's gutsy and he makes me smile. Then again, I ain't much of a father type, 'cause I'm too unbuttoned and I'd be a bad example.

The more I try to sleep the worse it gets. I hear Gabriel moving some too, and suddenly he whispers, "Duncan?"

"Go back to sleep," I says.

"You can't sleep either, huhn."

"Guess not."

"Why don't you sleep on the bed instead of the floor?"

"And what about you?"

"There's room enough."

I ain't crazy about the idea, but I give up trying to sleep on the couch cushions, and get back in my own bed. Gabriel makes himself comfortable right close to me, puts his head on my arm. He feels warm. I hug my arm around him and put my face into his hair, and he smells of soap and kid sweat. I can feel him breathing regular, like he's about to fall asleep again, and I don't know what makes me do it, but I kiss him on his head.

By the time the sky starts to lighten, I realize I'm still awake without a wink. I shut my eyes once more. Next thing I know, I'm wide awake from a dream. My heart is pounding hard and I'm remembering everything. I was dreaming that the cops had me against a wall with some other guys, and they had Gabriel blindfolded. They made him come close to the bunch of us. One cop asked the kid who did it, and he pointed to me and said, "He did it, I could tell because of the gasoline smell."

I'm real worried now, and I wish I never did sleep. I get up and get my pants on. I fish in my pocket and find the bank receipt, and then I look in my cash drawer to see I have only a couple hundred bucks there. It's my last day of playing Santa Claus.

Gabriel is still asleep, so I don't put on my shoes. I go in the bathroom and fill up the tub with hot water, and while that's doing I shave. I keep wondering if the ransom is gonna be delivered and what I might have to do if it ain't. Ransom, ransom—it's like a car alarm going off all day. I drop my razor and it hits my foot—lucky I'm not cut. When I'm done shaving, I brush my teeth two times and brush my tongue too, so it don't taste like an old sponge. By and by the tub is full enough, and I close the door and get in.

Looking out the window, I see a black bird flying around in a circle. It's bad luck, I think as I wash. I try not to look back out, but something keeps me wanting to check for that buzzard. I wash some more and suddenly I hear the kid's feet. He knocks. "Can you hurry?"

I stand up and pull the towel around me, then tell him to come in. "You going to help me finish the puzzle today, Duncan?" he asks.

"Yeah, I'll help."

"Good."

"You wet the bed?"

"Almost, but I woke up and ran, so none got on your bed." He looks at me standing there in the bath with a towel around me. His camouflage pajamas don't look so new, and the hole in the knee don't do a thing for them.

"Go get dressed, now. I'll take your dirty stuff to the laundry so you can have clean things to take home."

"When will I go, tonight?"

"Yeah, maybe." I look out the window, and the bird is gone. Now I wonder if I really saw it, or if it was just my imagination. "Hey, Gabriel, pull down that shade for me, willya?"

"How come? It lets the light in—"

"Just pull it halfway, you always gotta ask questions?"

He pulls the shade and goes out. When I'm done with my

bath, I go in the kitchen and see breakfast already on the table. Kid has scrambled eggs and toast and even coffee set out, I can smell it strong as soon as I open the door.

He comes out of my room with his pajamas and bed sheets wrapped in a bundle, and he drops them by the door and then sits down on his side of the table. "I'm not sick today, I feel real good." He looks out the window. "You think it's going to snow?"

"Ain't there enough?" I sit down in my seat and look at my plate. "Hey, thanks for cookin' this. Where'd you learn?"

"I make breakfast sometimes at home, because cereal gets boring and I like the smell of cooking."

The eggs taste kinda crunchy, but I don't tell him that. And the coffee tastes like it got scorched, kinda like tobacco juice, but I force it down anyhow. Scorched coffee and crunchy eggs—a great way to start off the day that could end up being my last.

Gabriel's full of pep. He swallows down his eggs, toast and milk, and then gets some Cap'n Crunch and eats that, too. Afterwards, he gets up and puts on the tree lights and some music on the stereo, grabs a couple of Nora's cookies, then runs back to the table and sits, pouring himself another glass of milk.

"You keep goin' like that and you're gonna throw up again," I says.

"Don't worry, I'm okay." He eats the cookies and drinks half the milk, then goes in the den.

When I'm doing the dishes, I look in and see him working over the puzzle. The picture is starting to come together except for a few spots where I can see big spaces. The box cover has a painting of a bunch of kids skating on a pond somewhere in the countryside, says it's from Grandma Moses.

He looks up at me quick, then back down. "Come on, Duncan. I want to get this done today."

"Yeah, sure, Gabriel." I get down on the floor and help him put some pieces together.

"You know," he says, "I keep thinking about what fun I'll have when I get home. I'm starting to really miss my mom and dad, too."

"Don't count on it yet," I says. I look at my watch and see it's almost ten, time to hit the street. I'm nearly cockeyed from the puzzle, anyways. I get up and tie the kid's leg to the chain, and he acts like he don't even care. "I gotta go to work," I says. "See you at supper."

"You think I can finish the puzzle?"

"Yeah, finish it up." I throw a few of my clothes and some used towels in with the laundry bundle, grab my Santa stuff and leave. On my way down the stairs, I think about what I have in my pocket. Gabriel don't know he'll never finish the puzzle today, because I snitched a piece of it. I'll be the one who finishes the puzzle.

Outside is good weather, it's not too cold and not too warm, either. It's cloudy enough, and I can see it might snow. I stop off in the laundry and get the girl to take care of the clothes for me.

\*   \*   \*

At lunchtime on my Santa Claus corner, all sorts of stuff is going on. There's a group of Chinese kids from Chinatown, they all get in a circle and sing some Christmas songs for me. It's a big help, because more people stop to listen to them and so I get more money. Teenage kids come by here and there. To be honest, I think they like Santa Claus just as much as little kids do. I'm busy shaking hands with the Chinese kids in the little choir, and I notice Martina, the art girl, standing nearby with her big folder, watching. I stop in the middle of shaking a small girl's hand and stand up straight.

Martina is looking right at me, and when she sees I'm looking at her, she smiles. "They could get you a job at the North Pole," she says.

"Long as it's part-time," I says.

"You know, I'm just going to set up over there and do my thing. I just want to draw you before I don't get another chance. Do you mind?"

"Me? Oh, just help yourself." I follow her with my eyes as she begins to set up. Then I get shaking hands again. After the Chinese kids go on, I see my pot is getting pretty stuffed. Soon, I take out the bills and fold them up, stuff them in my boot. I'm starting to get hungry, but I don't have the heart to leave while she's drawing me. For almost another half-hour, I ring my bell and keep ho-ho-hoing, collecting a good take. Next time I look over, Martina's sketching away. She's got this studious look, and she's kinda working her lip over with her teeth. She eyes me, then smiles. Then she picks up the sketch and brings it over to me.

I sure wasn't expecting to see myself the way she drew me. Somehow she got Santa Claus to look exactly like me. "I want this for myself," she says. "You don't mind, do you?"

"Sure, you can keep it," I says.

"Can I ask you something?"

"Me? Sure."

"What's better, lunch or dinner?"

I look at her dimple and her dancing eyes, and I says, "You mean for me personally, or in general?"

"You—personally."

"I'd have to say dinner. Lunch is just eat and run, mostly, you know. Kinda—quick. But dinner, you can relax and stuff."

"Oh…" She stands there looking at me for a while. "Well,

I guess I better put this away so it doesn't get damaged." She takes the sketch and puts it into her big folder. "I'm pretty hungry now, so I'm going to grab a bite. If I don't see you, have a Merry!"

"Yeah—you too. Merry Christmas, yourself!" I watch as she walks away and is soon gone.

Now it's time for a break. I go in the restaurant where I can sit in the window. Somehow if I keep busy as Santa Claus, I don't think much about the kidnapping or if it's going to work—or about Martina standing there smiling at me with that dimple, but seeming a hundred miles away. I sit near a window that has all snow and holly decorations on it, and lots of people stop and look as I eat.

After lunch the sky starts to get that cast iron gray look, and snow flurries come drifting on the air like white confetti. I drop in a card store and get Dick Murphy a card so I can have something to put his money in. I write, "Merry Christmas to you and yours. Duncan." While I'm there, I can hear the organ guy outside playing the most soulful music. He's a blind black guy, sings in cold or warm weather, always has a crowd listening to him. He's been around for years, and I see him lots of times, but I don't know his name. Kinda like me, I guess—people see me lots of times, but I don't think any of them know who I am. To them, I'm just another Santa Claus. Outside, I stop a minute to hear him sing, and a few people turn to eye me in my red suit. The organ guy sees nothing, he just keeps playing there in his big winter coat with the hood, his cash bucket at his feet under the keyboard. I walk away slow so I can hear the rest of his song, looking up to the sky to see if I can tell how high up it is when you can start to see snowflakes fall. No way, I think. That's one of them things that can't be done.

Back at my corner, the kidnapping thing hits me full force. Today is the day. I feel the sweat start to come, and my lunch ain't settling too well. I could be rich tomorrow, or I could be in jail. Or even worse, I could be shot down dead. What happens to me and the kid if the ransom never gets paid? I know I ain't about to hurt him or anything, but I was never in a kidnapping before and don't have a plan for that. Then I wonder what it would be like if I kept him as my own and moved far away?

I tell myself to calm down and keep cool, 'cause it's the cool people who stay out of trouble. There is always another day to get the money. It'll just have to be later that the kid gets to go home.

Every minute takes forever to pass, and it seems like the whole city is in slow motion like in a movie. By and by I hear the church bell ring three times, and I keep on the lookout for Dick Murphy. Right now he's the important one. I have fifty dollars in his envelope, ready to hand to him. Meanwhile, I keep ringing the bell, not paying attention to how much money is getting tossed in the pot.

Snow is falling regular now, dusting over everything. Up and down the street I stretch my neck and stand on tiptoes to see if Dick is coming along.

No Dick Murphy. I take the bills out of my beggar pot and fold them into my boot, jingle the change a little, then look out over the street again. I'm about ready to pack up and go for the money myself, but something tells me to stay a little longer.

# TAPE EIGHTEEN

Around three-thirty, I feel my insides getting tight and cold. My stomach's making noises, and I try to drown them out with bell ringing. Shivering, I have to keep my jaw clamped so my teeth don't chatter. I can't even think up a thought. My brain is stuck on the ding-a-ling, ding-a-ling, ding-a-ling.

A tap on my shoulder zaps me 200 volts. I spin around and see Dick Murphy, dressed in dirty broken down clothes, mangy work boots. "Whoa!" I says. "Don't sneak up on Santa Claus like that."

"Sorry I'm late—I just got off work. Christmas Eve and we work a whole day. I got plaster in my hair, up my nose and down my underwear."

He looks like a bag man, and he's even carrying a brown shopping bag with handles. "What's in the bag?" I ask.

"My clothes—I didn't have time to change."

"Sorry about that, chief," I says. "I usually change in the dressing room across the street, if you want—"

"Later, later on, Santa. Remember, I'm only gonna be scroungin' in the bushes, anyways."

"Great show, Murph. Now remember, the bag should be in them bushes just like I told you. If it ain't there, just take a walk around the place and then look again."

"Don't worry, old boy. You act like you're pretty worried."

"Ahm—I should be. It's the first time I ever had to deliver the charity to the bank."

"Come on, nobody'll bother you."

"It ain't me I worry about. Last year a guy got trailed, and they stole the money. If you think you're being trailed, duck in the stores and get lost."

"Okay, okay, nothin' to get uptight about."

"You better go make that pickup now. I'm startin' to get pretty cold."

He looks at me funny. "So who says you gotta stay out here all night? Meet me in a store."

"Store?"

"Yeah, say Filene's. Stay in the Santa suit, I'll find you easier." Murph skips onto the street with his bag of clothes and disappears in the crowd of last-minute shoppers.

I don't know how my talk sounded to Dick Murphy, but it sounded like hash to me. I'm so nervous I get the shakes and shivers. Lots can go wrong. If the money is in them bushes, some sharp cops are going to have a trail on it. I know for sure they ain't about to let that cash sit there without at least a few pairs of eyes hawking at it. And if it ain't there—I don't even want to think about that.

I ring my bell full swing now, and call, "Ho-Ho-Ho! Remember the needy on Christmas Eve!" I feel a lot of pressure in my head. Here I am standing on top of a hundred thousand bucks, but it's as far away from me as Fort Knox ever was, till I get it in my own hands.

Pretty soon I'm so wrapped up that I'm barely jingling my bell, and I'm counting each snowflake that hits my beggar pot. I already got done counting all the dimes with my eyes, then the nickels, then the quarters that show around the dollar bills. By and by I hear the four o'clock bells ringing. My jaw is clenched, and shivers are creeping through me.

A cruiser with two cops in it drives past me and pulls to the side up ahead, and the cops stay inside. Down the other way is a cop on horseback. It's almost dark now, so I can't see what they're doing.

I'm looking up and down the street, hoping to catch sight of Dick Murphy, but I see that even with the store lights, it's hard to tell one person from another unless they're right near-by. Now I'm thinking, if Murph shows up here, there could be big trouble. If he gets bagged, he's gonna get grilled about the kidnapping. He'll find out I used his friendship and lied to him on top of being a lowlife kid stealer. My heart bangs in me, and my head is making a terrible noise. If I wasn't so cold, I might just break out and run away. It ain't the right time or place for a drop, there's a big trap—if there are three cops showing uniform, there must be another bunch in plain clothes all around.

Usually by this time I'm packing up my Santa Claus stuff and heading home. But I figure to wait till I can be sure Murph is at Filene's. My bell ringing and ho-hoing ain't doing much good now, since most people are hurrying home from the stores and pass right by. The street is busy, pretty under the falling snow. The cop car is still parked up ahead, though I can't spot that cop on horseback. I start to feel panicky, and the cold has my feet about solid as marble now. I bang them out on the sidewalk.

Next thing I know, I see Dick Murphy dressed in his regular clothes, walking straight toward me from across the street. He has two shopping bags now, and I see he has a fancy wrapped gift on top of one. Nobody's following him, and I don't see any activity from the cops. Murph says, "I thought we were supposed to meet in Filene's."

"I was just on my way," I says. "I didn't think you'd be so fast."

"Fast?" he laughs. "I went in Filene's and didn't find you, so I changed my clothes and looked for you again, and still you weren't there, so I went and found you a little present."

"No kiddin'," I says. "Everything all set?"

"Oh yeah, no problem. At first I couldn't tell where you meant, 'cause it was starting to get dark. But I found it. I gotta get moving though, Eileen's waiting for me."

I ring the bell some more, still fidgety somebody might be on to us. "Thanks a million, Murph. Oh—hang on, I got your candy cane here." I pull out his envelope and a candy cane, and stick them in his coat.

"Aw gee, Duncan. You didn't have to do that—but I'm glad you did," he says.

"Sure thing—we should keep in touch."

"Call me up. I'm the only Dick under Murphy," he laughs. "Have a nice one, Duncan. And keep outa trouble."

"Good goin'," I says. "Thanks again." I watch him take off down the street and blend in with the crowd and the falling snow. Looking at the shopping bag next to my legs, I figure the sooner I get off the street, the better. I take the bills out of my pot and fold them in my boot. Then I grab the pot and the shopping bag and head into the store for changing. By the big wall clock, I see it's quarter of five.

In the dressing room I get out of my Santa suit in a flash, stuff it all in the Santa suit bag. Now I notice the bottom of the ransom bag is wet. The announcement comes over the speaker that the store will be closing in ten minutes, and for all the customers to head for the cashiers with their purchases.

My hands are trembling. I lift the gift box out of the shopping bag and see two bank bags inside, one with a flap and one with a zipper. I peek in the one with the flap, and my heart pounds in me and my mouth goes dry. I never seen so much money, all in them phony looking new hundreds and fifties. Quickly I cover both the bank bags with my Santa suit bag, then top it off with my gift box. Last of all I put all my charity change in my money bag and stick it down my pants for safe keeping.

I know why I ain't jumping around and screaming. It ain't only because I'm afraid I could still have a cop on my tail, but it's mostly because I don't really believe I'm walking around with all this money. It don't seem real. I guess I never really thought I could pull it off. Maybe if I really believe it's just shopping I got in the bag, then I won't get in trouble. I look in the mirror and rub off the red on my cheeks and nose. Then I go out of the dressing room and pick up a fancy shopping bag for a half a buck, stuff the damp bag inside the new one, and shove on out of there.

\*     \*     \*

By now it's completely dark and the snow is letting up. I'm glad everything came out smooth so far. I have this jittery feeling that I'm being followed, though. I know that if I go straight to my apartment, I could set off a bomb of cops under myself if a single one is on my trail.

I walk down Washington Street, get the blood moving in my feet. Some church bells are ringing "Angels We Have Heard on High" in the distance. For Christmas Eve there's still a lot of people around, and I feel safer in the crowd. Cutting through

Chinatown, I come to the bus terminal in South Station, and I duck in there with the bag. The wall lockers are almost all used up, but I find two that are open. I lift out Murph's present and my Santa outfit, then I shove the ransom money in the locker and shut the door. I put the key in my pocket, take my things and go. As I'm leaving, I think to open the present. It's the first one I got in years. I pull off the wrapping and open the box, and inside is a plaid scarf from Scotland. I unfold the scarf and wrap it around my neck, toss the wrapping in a trash can.

Now I think about Gabriel. He's waiting at my place for me, probably hungry by now. I think of how I'd have nothing today if it wasn't for him. A creepy feeling comes in my stomach. I realize I still have to get the kid home, because my part of the deal ain't done. I walk real fast, try to find a pay phone. Finally I spot one, fiddling in my pockets to find the number. In one pocket is the locker key with my other keys, in another is that puzzle piece I snitched from Gabriel, and in the back pocket down under my wallet I find the crumpled up scrap with Old Win Booker's number on it. I pick up the phone and start to dial, but then I put it back down again. I can't think of a way to say thank you and screw you at the same time, but I sure can make him squirm for a couple more hours.

*   *   *

The walk home is long and cold. I pass the laundry and remember to pick up the clothes, and just in time, too. The girl has her coat on and is chewing me out for keeping her late on Christmas Eve, so I give her five extra bucks for a tip. When I get home, I see I got my ATM card in the mailbox. I put that right in my wallet. Then I go up the stairs, feeling good to be home and still alive. I open the door and find Gabriel standing behind it, angry as a stung rooster. "What's the big idea?" he says.

"What big idea?"

"Why'd you have to go send my mother that tooth? I saw it on the television." He stands away from me and puts his hands on his hips.

I look at him, then shove the laundry in his arms. "It was the only way I could get you home safe," I says, and I walk out of the kitchen into my bedroom. I put my Santa suit bag up on the closet shelf.

He comes to the bedroom door and drops the laundry onto his couch cushions. "Did you get the money? Did my dad pay?"

"Everything's okay," I says. I take the chain key out and unlock his ankle, and he lifts his foot and rubs it all around. I move him back in the kitchen under that bird mobile he made, and I rub my hand through his hair. "You'll get to be home for Christmas."

He shouts out and jumps up in my arms, his eyes all shiny with happiness. While I'm holding him, I feel the money bag in my pants go loose, and then it slips down my leg. Halfway down my leg, the coins start to spill.

"You've got a hole in your pocket," the kid says.

I put him down and he stands back. "The hell I do."

He looks at the flood of money pouring down my leg and over the kitchen linoleum like a jackpot. He just stands there watching, then looks at me puzzled. I stand there too, and don't say a word. His face clouds up. His mouth moves a little, then he looks again at the money. "That's the ransom?" he asks.

"No, it ain't," I says just as quick. "It's from my work. Now help me pick it up."

We pick up the money and put it in the drawer next to my bed. "Where's the ransom?"

"Kid, you talk too much. I got it stashed in a safe place."

"Oh."

Looking around, I see the kid has the place all clean. He has my bed made and the couch cushions lined up on the floor with the blankets folded on them. The kitchen floor is washed and the sink has no dirty dishes in it. The tree lights are on and the whole place looks ready for company. On the den floor is that puzzle.

"I see you got the puzzle done," I says. He sits down on the couch without the cushions and rubs his ankle again, then looks at the puzzle.

"There's a piece missing," he says. "I looked all over the place and couldn't find it."

"Did you look under the tree real good?" I ask.

"I looked everywhere," he says, and he gets down on his belly and looks under the Christmas tree, anyhow.

I take the piece out of my pocket. "Oh, I found it!" I says. Gabriel shimmies up fast and looks at me while I'm showing it to him. Then I put the piece on the puzzle and it's done.

"Where'd you find it?" he says. "I already looked all over this room twice and couldn't find it. Where'd you find it? Tell me."

"In my pocket."

He looks at me and tips his head, putting his hands on his hips. I look back at him the same way, and put my hands on my hips. "I put the last piece in, I finished the puzzle," I says, and I stick my tongue out at him.

"Aargh! You cheated, you cheater." He darts both hands into the top of my pockets. "What else are you hiding?" he says, and I try to pull away because it tickles me and feels way too personal.

I grab his hands and pull them out. Then I twist him around and give him a tickling on his sides, and he drops to the floor laughing. He squirms back around and looks up at me, his face as bright and fresh with life and laughter as anything I've ever seen. For a long time we just look at each other's faces, eye to eye, and I feel something like I'm passing through a minute of heaven, like I'm always going to have this for as long as I live.

We both stand back up, and he pats down the front of his rumpled shirt. "So big deal," he says. "I did most of the work."

I turn away and put a tape in the player. When I turn back, Gabriel is sitting on the couch looking at the puzzle picture and fiddling with the end of the chain. I take the chain away from him and unravel it from around the heat pipe. Then I wrap it up and throw it back under the couch where it used to be. "You feel like eatin'?"

"I thought you were never going to come back," he says. "I'm almost starved."

I make the kid watch some TV while I make our supper. He looks at cartoons every day, and every time I hear him laugh with that tickled laugh of his, I peek in the doorway of the den to see what's funny. Then I hear him change the channel a few times, and on comes some Christmas music. Suddenly he shouts out, "Hey look, this is my friend, Justin! There it is, they're showing the Christmas Revels. I was supposed to go see this."

I go in the room and stand over him, put my hands on his shoulders. "Sorry you had to miss out on stuff."

"I don't mind, Duncan. At least I'm seeing it. Look, that's Justin right there."

Justin is singing in front, a solo, and the rest of the singers join in a carol I never heard before. The show continues while I get supper done. For a Christmas Eve special we have spaghetti with mushrooms and roasted red peppers, and we watch the show while we eat. After that we turn off the TV and put on the music I bought. I set out some ice cream and root beer for a sort of Christmas party. Gabriel mashes his ice cream and whips it up to look like a Dairy Queen. Then he lifts up his root beer glass and holds it in the air in front of me, and so

I lift mine up too, and we clink them together. "Merry Christmas to a jolly good fellow," he says, and I says, "To a jolly good fellow yourself."

He's full of talk tonight. When he says something about things he likes, his eyebrow goes up a little on one side. He tells me about how he loves to go sledding, and about how good he is at playing hockey, and about his cousins and friends, and about how one time he and his mom built a huge igloo that four people and a dog could fit in. Between talking, he keeps getting up to change the music.

"There can't be too many kids that have an adventure like I had, huhn Duncan," he says.

"Nope."

"I want to tell people what it's like to get kidnapped."

"Oh, no you don't," I says. "You don't tell nobody. You don't want people thinkin' it's any good to get kidnapped. Most of the time it ends up with somebody dead or in jail. You want people to come after me and throw me in jail?"

He looks at his dish of ice cream. "No."

"Well, then," I says. "Don't tell a soul. Tell them whoever stole you kept you blindfolded all the time, and you never knew what was happenin'."

"But it's too much of an adventure not to tell someone."

"What about the hitchhiking part? And skipping school? You gonna tell everybody about that, too?"

"Duhh, I don't think so! Some stuff you can never tell."

"Well then, just wait a year or so before you open your trap. I'll be long gone outa town by then."

"You're going to leave town?"

"Yeah, probably right after you go home."

"Well, what happens if I want to run away again? Can I come here to stay?"

"You ain't gonna run away. You got friends there and you gotta stick with them. Your father's a real square guy and he don't want to lose you, and your mother was a wreck all week about you gettin' kidnapped. So you got your own place to stay."

"But can't I come to see you? We're almost like friends now."

"No. And tell me somethin', while I'm thinkin' about it. How come you really ran away from home?"

He looks at me with them eyes, and I look right back at him. "I sort of told you before," he says. "It's because my mom and dad wouldn't let me go on the Polar overnight. My dad said he wasn't crazy about the staff, and excuses like that. But I knew he didn't want me to go because I wet the bed."

"So, they don't like you to wet the bed then," I says.

"I dunno. Probably they do like it, because then they can keep me from doing stuff like other kids."

"Oh, I doubt that," I says.

"Oh, yeah? How do you think you got to kidnap me?"

"Tell you the truth, I had three different plans—and none of them had you running away from home. Besides, what else would you do, wet the bed at somebody's house?"

"No—I'd use my sleeping bag on an air mattress, just like when I ran away last summer. Then in the morning I'd just roll it up and take it home for the laundry. Or now, I would use one of the Good Nites like you bought me."

"So what it comes down to, is you ran away to punish your dad."

He don't say anything for a while, then he shrugs and looks down at his dish. "I guess," he says. "I didn't think he would ever pay the ransom."

"Well, he did pay the ransom. Besides, it looks to me like you won't be wettin' the bed much longer, anyways. You're growing out of it, so pretty soon your folks'll let you do more stuff."

His eyebrow goes up and he nods. "Probably. But can't I come to visit you some time?"

"No. N-o-u-g-h. If you see me on the street that's okay, but you don't dare come lookin' for me—you'll have me bagged."

He looks at his dish again. "Okay," he says, and he stays quiet for the rest of his ice cream.

# TAPE NINETEEN

I planned to get the kid a taxi home right after supper, but with all our talk it's after ten, and he says he don't mind staying over as long as he can get home first thing in the morning. I know right well it's gonna crack his parents inside out not to get him right away, now that the ransom's paid. But I'm getting a little power trip, knowing he wants to stay with me. So I set my alarm for five o'clock. He wants to surprise his folks on their doorstep around seven. Come time for him to sleep, I get him one of them Good Nites. "Here," I says. "Why don't you get your pajamas on and brush your teeth."

He takes the liner and looks at it, then he looks at me.

"Can I try sleeping without it?"

"You think it's a good idea?"

"I don't know. I want to try."

"Then go ahead."

He goes in the bathroom to get changed, and I set out his clothes so he can get them on first thing in the morning.

"Can you keep the Christmas lights on all night?"

"What for?" I ask. "How you gonna see 'em if you're sleepin'?"

"But Duncan, you don't understand."

"Okay, so I'll leave 'em on all night."

"Thanks." He smiles, almost to himself.

"You forgot to say your prayers last night, Gabriel. Come on, let's say 'em now."

He pats the sides of his pajama pants and looks at me. "Feels a lot better without that diaper," he says. Then he kneels on the floor next to my bed while I sit on the bed to listen.

"Now I lay me down to sleep," he says, and he thinks for a while. I'm almost ready to tell him what comes after, but he remembers. "I pray the Lord my soul to keep." He looks at me.

"Good," I says. "Go on."

"And if I die—and if I die before I wake." He looks at me again, and I fold my arms to wait. "And if I die before I wake, ahm—wake me up," he says. It ain't the way I taught him, but it'll have to do. I have him go back to the couch cushions now that he ain't sick anymore, and pretty soon he's sound asleep.

Now to act out my plan—Christmas Eve is as good a night as any to pick up the ransom and get it back here safe. The Santa Claus suit is the secret, I think as I change into some long underwear. With that suit on, people will see I'm just packing off to a party, like a costume ball or something. Anybody sees me carrying the ransom money around, they'll see it's just a shopping bag, nothing suspicious.

It's a foolproof idea, and I hurry to get into my shirt and my heavy leather coat. After that I put on the Santa Claus suit. I do it all up as fancy as I ever done. The beard is perfect and big and fluffed out, and the wig is on tight so none of my own hair shows. I put the red on my cheeks and nose, and white powder in my eyebrows. Then I wash my hands and pull on the black boots and white gloves.

I check in my pocket and see I got the locker key. To make sure it doesn't get lost, I tie it on a piece of string and then tie the string to a belt loop on my pants. Now I can make the ransom pickup safe as a baby. Even if I get bagged by the cops, I can get out of it pretty quick and tell them I don't know nothing about no kidnapping, but some bookie gave me the key to the locker and paid me to pick up some money for him.

I go down the stairs to my car and open the trunk. Grabbing the shopping bags, I make sure none of the kid's toys fall back in the trunk, then I swing the lid closed. The big bag I throw over my shoulder, and the other one I carry at my side. The wind is pretty icy now, and the outside is quiet except for a few people walking. I use my foot to open the front door and hustle inside, so the door don't close on the bags. I climb up the three flights of hollow stairs and go real quiet into my house.

In the den the lights are twinkling away and the place is peaceful, rich with the smell of pine. I take the toy bags and drop them on the floor, then sit on the couch without the cushions. For a long time I watch the lights twinkle, thinking about how this week went. More has happened in these days than in the past ten years. I got a Christmas tree and a stereo and decorations, and even a kid to give stuff to like other folks—and also a present from good old Dick Murphy.

I think about how happy Gabriel will be when he takes a look at the toys. Lifting myself off of the couch and tiptoeing across the kitchen, I look in on him. He sleeps neater than me—the couch cushions are all together under him, and he's sleeping on his stomach with his hand mushed up under his cheek. I tiptoe back in the den and start to get the toys out of the bags. I don't have them wrapped, but it's just as well. He'll see right off that the gifts are his.

Underneath the tree it looks like a toy shop. Suddenly it

dawns on me that the kid's going to be lugging all this stuff home, and what's he doing with a couple of sacks of toys coming home from a kidnapping? He could always say Santa Claus left them, which would probably rile up his parents because it ain't the Santa Claus they know. But I ain't ready to get caught with my red pants down. If I get seen picking up the ransom in my Santa suit, and then the kid brings home a pile of gifts from Santa Claus, then the cops could put two and two together. They'll call it the Santa Claus kidnap caper and set the big guns to hunt me down. So I better not tell the kid a single thing about Santa Claus, not even to joke. He'll just have to say the kidnappers bought him toys to keep him from causing trouble, and he somehow got to take them home. They'll have to believe him, because what else could they come up with better than that?

* * *

The car is cold and can't start. I keep cranking it and cranking it, but the fool thing just whines and clicks out. After I try it about fifteen times, I give up. I'm dressed good enough for the cold, so I walk fast, and pretty soon I'm right in town near the bus terminal.

A couple of old, broken down guys are walking toward me, both of them pretty drunk, and one of them toothless. They stop in front of me, look at me with them hungry eyes you see a lot of in the city at night. "Oh-ho-ho, Merry Christmas," I says. The two old guys laugh noisily and cut off down an alley.

By and by I'm at the terminal. A bus is letting out people, and they're the only ones around except for the few loners still traipsing the streets. A couple cars and taxicabs stop and pick up the people from the bus. Meanwhile, I go to my locker humming Christmas tunes, and some people smile. A little girl with a Southern accent takes her camera and snaps me, tells the old lady she's with that she never saw such a dandy Santa Claus before. I says ho-ho-ho to them, and take out my key.

Before I open my locker I turn and check all around, see if there's any cops. There's nobody but the folks just off of the bus, and a security guard keeping an eye on luggage. One old sleepy-headed fat guy is behind the desk paying the place no attention. Feeling pretty safe, I open the locker and get out the shopping bag.

# TAPE TWENTY

As I walk home, I hear some shuffling fast and confused on the sidewalk behind me. Before I can turn my head, I feel an arm come up around my throat. I try to pull away, see who it is, but whoever it is must be a moose. Then I see two other big guys come around in front of me, and they're both black. The guy behind me says, "If it ain't my old pal, Santa Claus. You're the sucker that almost got me arrested."

"How's that?" I says. I squirm out of the guy's grip and try to get away, but then one of the guys in front pulls out this knife that ain't big, but sure looks sharp.

"Remember me an' my midget?" he says from behind, and I can't see what he looks like, but I can figure pretty easy who he is.

"Why, am I supposed to remember you?" I ask.

"Give up de cash," says one of the guys in front.

"Okay, okay," I says. I put the shopping bag down on the sidewalk and start in my pocket for some money. I pull out twenty-five dollars and some change, then I show them I have no more money in my pockets, just my keys.

"That all, Mister Santa Claus?" the guy behind me says, like he don't believe me.

"Yeah, yeah, that's all I got, honest," and I show the pockets again. I try to turn around, but then he jams a fist in my back and says don't move, so I stay still. "That's all I got," I says. "I'm just goin' to a costume party, so I ain't carryin' much."

"Get the bag," he says to the two black guys in front of me, and when they go for the bag, a hot rush runs through me. My arm shoots around and I jam my elbow right in the guy's jewels behind me. He goes over halfway and starts groaning and swearing.

The guy with the little razor knife is right at me, now. He slices my arm and I can hear my leather coat hiss, and I can feel blood run down my arm. I kick him, and his little knife flies out of his hand and skids off of the sidewalk like a silverfish. Then I punch him about six good hard ones right across his bumpy face and on the neck and under the chin. I hurt my knuckles on his chin or his teeth, I can't see exactly which I'm hitting. Then I bash his nose, and watch him go down on the ground with blood coming out of his nose like a faucet.

The other black guy grabs me around my throat. He's powerful, and he has a hateful look. I see from the side that the moose I elbowed in the nuts is coming at me again, too, this time with a razor knife he pulled on me the other day. I break out of the hold and grab the shopping bag, run as fast as I can.

Turns out the moose is faster. He comes up behind me and grabs me by the Santa suit, and I hear it rip wide. I'm still trying to get away because I see I'm outnumbered and outknifed. The black guy scrambles around a car to the front of me and don't wait a second, he starts right in with his fists. He goes for my face, but I duck and crouch down low, and back away against the car. Then he comes down on my back with the both of his fists like a sledge hammer. I fall on the ground, feeling like I can't breathe. My Santa suit is all mud and snow now, and I don't worry about that no more. I just worry about the money.

The big moose starts to kick me in the side and in the back, and I don't take that from nobody. I grab a hold of his foot and pull myself up while pushing him back, and he staggers a little. He kicks his foot free, and then I'm halfway up and I ram my fist. It goes right between his knees, and he jumps back without a sound. I'm ready to jump up on him and finish him off, but I see the black guy is off with my ransom.

I take off after him, and I rush him in a corner. I feel the blood still running from the cut on my arm. I know I got more to lose, so I'm gonna fight harder. I tell him to put the bag down and get away with the twenty-five bucks, before he don't get away with nothing. He starts to put the bag down, but then I see him look out past my shoulder quick.

Before I even get a chance to look around and see what he looked at, I get a kick behind my knees. I spin around, and it's the big moose. "What the hell is this?" I says.

"Sucker," he says to me, and he pulls out a knife and starts to cut at me right through my clothes. "I'm gonna gut you like a fat fish," he says.

The black guy yells, "Let's just go, man!"

But the moose has me against the corner now, and there ain't much I can do, he's going so fast. He's knifing for my chest again and again, and I manage to keep pushing his hand off so he can't get a straight stab. I want to fall down and fake like I'm dead so he'll take off, but I want to make him pay for this even more.

With all my strength I ram my head in his face. I see stars and taste tin foil in my mouth. I feel like I'm walking on an overstuffed electric mattress. My knees give way, and I feel myself going down on the ground. I don't go out, but everything stays fuzzy for a minute as I keep trying to get up.

In a while I can see straight enough to know my head is pretty hard, because the moose is decked out on the sidewalk. I get up slow and look around for my bag, but it's gone. The guy who ripped it off is gone, too. I start to run for it, but I feel too weak to go far, and I don't even know if I'd be going the right way. My head is pounding and I look down at myself, see if I'm okay. There's about six cuts on my chest. They ain't too deep because my clothes are thick, but they're bleeding heavy and the cold wind makes them feel very wet.

The moose is starting to pick himself off of the ground. I walk over to him and look at his face. His nose is all bent out of shape from me banging my head against him, and he has a couple broken teeth, but other than that he ain't too bruised. When he's halfway up I says, "You lowlife," and I kick him real hard right below his chest. He arches over and I close up both his eyes with a few fast punches. "And give this to your midget friend," I says, and I bash my fist on the side of his face so hard my whole arm gets numb. He groans and falls over sideways, whacking his head against a trash bin, and I leave him there in the gutter like his bumpy-faced friend. Nobody street fights with me and walks away, either they fall or they run.

I stand still for a minute, rubbing my hand to see if it's broken. Slowly, I look around. Down the way is the bumpy-faced guy still on the ground, and he'll be there a while. In front of me is the moose. Not bad for three against one, except the third guy is the one with the ransom money. He'll be a surprised son of a gun to find out what he's got in that bag.

I look down at myself. My Santa Claus suit is all shreds, and full of blood and dirt. My white gloves are torn up and there's blood all over them, too. On the ground are my Santa hat and wig. I pick them up and put them on as good as I can, using a store window for a mirror.

I'm never gonna see that money, no matter what. I could never track it down without leaving myself wide open, either. I should've known this couldn't be so easy. This is how I pay for bad ways, I think as I make for home—my whole plan destroyed before my eyes. All along I been thinking I was so smart to outwit the cops and to outwit everyone, and when it comes down to it I was pretty stupid. I should've never walked. As soon as I knew my car was dead, I should've just waited for another day. Now, my whole plan is gone to the dogs, and what I'm gonna do for my rent and food come spring, I ain't got the slightest notion. But I guess I had it coming, one way or another.

I keep looking around to see if that guy shows up with the shopping bag. It's just a dream, I think, to hope for him to show his face. I drag my feet one after the other until I'm at my front door, and I go in and make my way up the stairs.

# TAPE TWENTY-ONE

It takes a long time to get out of my clothes, I'm so beat up. My T-shirt sticks to the dried blood on my cuts, and I can see black and blues on my legs and arms. I see none of the cuts has to take a stitch, though the one on my arm is long and pretty deep. If I didn't have my leather coat on, I would've been in trouble.

I take out some bandages, and while I'm almost ready to put them on, I see I should first take a bath and get all the blood off of me. Real quiet I close the bathroom door and run the hot water. I put the top of the toilet seat down and sit on it while I wait.

Pretty soon the tub is full enough, and I strip off my underwear and sink in. The hot water feels good on me as I lie back with my knees in the air. When the water goes in my cuts it stings something fierce, but I get used to it and wash off. The water turns brownish red, like it's rusty. The cut on my arm is still letting a little blood out, but the rest ain't too bad. My eyes are so heavy, I feel like I want to fall asleep right in the hot water.

I still got to get Gabriel home in the morning. It ain't his fault I muffed up the whole operation. But after he's gone, I get to be myself again. When I think about that, I don't like the idea, and I feel strange. I don't want to be alone no more like I used to. It's so much better when you got someone around that you like and that likes you back.

I empty out the dirty water and fill the tub again, thinking about all that work and planning gone to the dogs. It's like so much else in my life. Soon as I think everything is gonna be all right, and I got it in the palm of my hand, then something blows it all away.

After I'm dried off and get some bandages on my cuts, I get into some clean underwear and a T-shirt for bed. I go in the den and look at the Christmas tree again, and look at the gifts for Gabriel underneath. The twinkling lights are still on, and I'm glad he talked me into leaving them on for the night.

I pack all my bloody clothes and Santa Claus stuff in a bag and stick it next to my trash. I keep my leather coat, because it's all I got for winter till I can get a new one. Finally, I go in my room and turn on the lamp by my bed. Then I look at Gabriel and see he's sound asleep. I sit on my bed and just watch the kid's face, wonder what he's dreaming about and what he wants to do when he grows up. He looks so peaceful there. I get up and go closer to him, lean over kinda achy so I can touch his face. He smiles in his sleep, and then he turns over.

Just as I sit on my bed again, he wakes up. He gets up on his elbow and squints over at me. "Duncan—Duncan, what happened to your arm and your legs?"

"Huhn?" I says.

"You got a bandage and all sores," he says, and he sits up on the couch cushions.

"I dunno. I got rolled outside."

His face looks horrified. "Who did it? My God, lookit the black and blues—Duncan, if I were you I'd go to the hospital."

"Go back to sleep kid, willya?" I says. "Just go to sleep and stop talkin' for once."

"Okay."

I shut my lamp and lie back to sleep. I hear Gabriel rustling in his covers, and the next thing I know, he's up and walking. I reach over and put on the lamp again. "What are you doin'?"

"I need to go to the bathroom," he says. He trips a little and has to hold onto the side of the doorway so he don't fall over.

"Hurry up, willya?" I says, and I lie back and try to sleep with the light in my face. After he's done, I hear him traipsing around with those feet pajamas. Suddenly he gasps, and he runs to me, stands right over my bed.

"Duncan—Duncan, did you get all those things under the Christmas tree? Was that you?"

I open my eyes slow, feeling almost dead. The kid's face looks too serious for me to brush him off, so I give him a kinda grin, and I says, "Yeah, I got 'em to keep you busy. Take 'em home with you."

He says thanks real happy and runs back in the den. In a minute he runs back and sits on my bed. He puts his arms around my shoulders and hugs me. "Thanks," he says. He hugs me for a long time, so I hug him back with my right arm that ain't too painful.

"You're a real pal, Duncan," he says with his face right next to mine.

"You are too, Gabriel."

He lifts his face and looks at me. I'm too tired to hug him anymore, so I let go. He says, "Are you sure you're never going to let me come and see you, not even in the summer or something?"

"Never," I says. "I'll only end up in jail."

"Oh." He hugs me tight again, and then he sits up and stares at me. His eyes change to cloudy. I look at myself to see what he's staring at, and I see my T-shirt has some blood on it that seeped through the bandages while he was hugging me. "Duncan, you even got your chest cut!"

"I know. I told you I got mugged. I'll be okay, just as long as you let me sleep." I pat his arm.

"You sure?"

"I'm sure. Please, I'm tired."

He gets off of my bed and goes back on his couch cushions, tucks himself in. "Good night, Duncan."

"Good night, Gabriel." I shut the lamp and fall back on my pillow to sleep like a dead man.

*    *    *

In the middle of the night, I wake up choking. I smell fire, and smoke is coming in the house. The hallway smoke alarm is wailing. My heart jumps in me and pounds like hell. I jump off of my bed and remember how beat up I am. I can hardly move, but I have to. I shove my loggy bruised legs in my pants and then put on my lamp. The smoke ain't too heavy, though it's leaking in steady along the baseboard right next to the kid's face. I run in the kitchen and put on the light, see there's more smoke coming in from under the door. There's no fire in my place, it must be downstairs.

Suddenly I remember the jug of gasoline, leaking all this time in the cellar, and I wonder if that started the fire. I rush in my room and shake the kid. He won't wake up, so I pick him up and put him on his feet. He falls right back down like a rag doll. I get dizzy, start coughing. "Oh Jesus, please don't let us die," I says. I grab him off of the floor and hold him up with my arm. He starts to wake up and he's coughing real rough, like his ribs are gonna split. I sit him on my bed. "Gabriel, we gotta get out, get your coat."

I grab a store bag and stick all my Santa Claus money in it from the dresser. "Come on, get the coat!" He don't get up, though, because he's coughing so hard he almost throws up. I get even more scared to think he has carbon monoxide poisoning.

I pull him off of the bed and get us both low on the floor for air. Then I drag him and the money bag along, figuring to go out the den fire escape. By the time we get to the window, the smoke is so thick I don't even try to save the new stereo. I fling open the window and shove the kid out on the fire escape in his pajamas. It's biting cold out there, and I see he'll need a blanket.

I get on the floor and scoot back in the kitchen on hands and knees. The Christmas tree goes dark, and the light on the kitchen ceiling flickers and turns orange, then it goes right out and leaves me bumping into things. I grab for my coat, and then I pull the blankets off of my bed and the couch cushions, and I scramble back to the den holding my breath. I see flames coming in the kitchen from the outside wall and under the door. Fire engines are screaming, but I know they're gonna be too late to save much.

I jump out the window to the fire escape, grab hold of the kid, who's still half knocked out and hacking, and hustle down the iron stairs with him and the money bag. Somehow I put three blankets around him as we make our way, but the money bag slips out of my hand and dumps open in the wind, and all my coins and dollar bills rain down on the pavement below.

Finally, we get down to the bottom of the fire escape, and I start to lean over to pick up some of the money. The wind is blowing the bills all over, and I'm too stiff to chase after them.

"Want me to help you?" the kid coughs.

I look at him standing there, ready to help me grub for nickels and dimes before he even has himself together. Suddenly I don't want any of it. "No," I says. "Let's go." I put my good arm over Gabriel and take him to a building across the street where a bunch of people are watching the fire from some wide cement steps. In the meantime some people see the money, and they go scrounging for whatever they can get, laughing and having a great time.

"Are you both all right?" somebody asks, and somebody else says, "Good goin', you made it." We both nod, and I try to get us blended with the people. I look over and see the whole two first floors under my apartment are burning up, and the third floor is starting to go strong. Some old lady says I'm the only one ain't got out yet, everybody else is safe. That's good to hear, I think. I sit down next to Gabriel and cough a little with him. He's good and wide awake now, and he looks at me with kind of a half smile, half cry. "I guess that's the end of my presents, huhn?"

"Yeah, that's the end of my house," I says.

Gabriel unwraps his blankets and opens them up. "Come on and sit under this," he says. I move closer and get wrapped up, and we watch the house burn. While we sit together, three cops all of a sudden show up in front of us. At first I don't think nothing of it, I just think they're out to investigate the fire. But they ain't asking no questions, they're just looking at Gabriel.

One of the cops says, "Are you Gabriel Booker?"

Gabriel looks at the cop, then at me. He blinks his eyes and looks down at the ground. He nods yes.

The other two cops come up the stairs right in front of everybody and grab me from my half of the blankets. They stand me up and I feel the long cut on my arm getting squashed in their grip. I try to pull loose, but I don't have no strength left. "What's goin' on here?" I says. "What's all this?"

"You're under arrest on suspicion of kidnapping Gabriel Booker, son of State Representative Winthrop—"

"What the hell are you sellin'?" I says and pull away. I stand back, see Gabriel has the bunch of blankets tight around him, and he's looking at me real scared. He coughs a few times, real raspy because he ain't got all the smoke out of him yet. "I don't know nothin' about this," I says, "and I'll tell you exactly what happened if you let me."

"Why don't we talk this over at the station," the tallest cop says.

"Why don't we?" I ask. "Because I don't belong in no cop station. Tonight I was drivin' home from a late show, and I see these three big guys tusslin' around with this little kid. I just slammed my car to a stop and jumped out. They were roughin' the kid up and I didn't know what they wanted. One guy said just get the money and screw the kid. Another one took out a knife and cut me up, so I had to deck him."

I stop when I see two of the cops looking at each other. "Where were these guys?" one asks me.

"Somewhere around South Station," I says. "Then the other guy tried to attack the kid and I gave it to him, too. But the first one took off—he had a shoppin' bag with him."

"They cut you up?" says the cop with the moustache.

I open my slashed coat, like he couldn't see for his own self, and lift up my T-shirt to show him the bandages right under it. "And that's what happened. I don't know nothin' about no kidnap," I says.

"I think we better hold off," says the tall cop real quiet to the one with the moustache. "They found those two guys up there all beat to hell..."

"I took the kid home with me," I says, and I see the cop with the moustache scribbling down what I say on his note pad. "You can see he's very shook up. He couldn't even tell me his name or address, so I just gave him some of my nephew's pajamas to wear, and put him to bed—figured I could get him home in the mornin'."

The three cops look at Gabriel and see he ain't quite himself. I know it's from breathing smoke, but they don't need to know that. Gabriel just sits there shivering under them blankets, still hacking a little here and there, still dazed.

"Try to go easy on the kid," I says. "He's pretty shook up."

The third cop is a heavy guy with a red, beefy face. He goes up close to the kid and talks real gentle, puts his hand under Gabriel's chin. "Is that what happened?" he says.

Gabriel nods and looks up at me. I'm standing on the top of the wide cement stairs, hoping to keep out of the frying pan. He stares at me for a while, then says, "He—he saved my life."

The cop looks at me and says, "Don't you realize you're obliged to report a crime, pal? You let time go by, and the investigation gets harder. Now, what's the story? You're all cut up, and you didn't call the police or go to a hospital emergency room?"

"I—I ain't got any insurance," I says. "I ain't hurt that bad, anyhow. I dunno. You're right, I shoulda called the cops. I was afraid of gettin' in trouble for fighting."

At the foot of the stairs there's all sorts of people, old folks and young, some watching the fire, some watching us. I hear one woman say, "That is Gabriel Booker, isn't it? He's a handsome fellow." Other people start to gossip about it, and before I know it a reporter comes by and starts taking pictures of Gabriel and the police and the firemen and everything. Another reporter steps in and starts asking the cops some questions. The cop with the moustache says, "We have Gabriel Booker in our protection, he's apparently safe and unharmed."

More reporters and camera people come by, scrambling over each other like sharks in bloody water. "What about the kidnapping, officer? Have you any statements about the kidnapping? Was the child molested?"

"We have no statements about any kidnapping," says the cop with the moustache. "It is under investigation."

I think now about an investigation. Even if the cops turn up the ransom money, and those three guys who mugged me go to court, nobody's ever going to find the Santa Claus that had the shopping bag of ransom. Santa Claus has his fancy outfit just about cooked in the fire by now.

*   *   *

The cops try to get Gabriel to wait in a cruiser for his parents, but he says three times he just wants to watch the fire. So I'm sitting next to him on the stairs, and we're watching the fire the best we can through the shoulders of the big cops standing in front of us, keeping the news people out of the kid's face. Pretty soon I see a big road barge pull up, and in a second I see it's that Expedition I saw in their garage last week. Gabriel don't even see his mother and father pile out of the SUV with some other guy that looks a little like Winthrop Booker himself. I nudge Gabriel and point down to the street. Well, I never seen the way that kid runs to his mother and father right in them camouflage pajamas. He kisses his mother about ten times and she kisses him the same, and they don't say nothing at all. The camera people are flashing the eyes out of everyone there, and I'm sure glad I ain't them. Then I see Gabriel jump up in Winthrop Booker's arms, and they hug and kiss for a while. Strange to think if the old man ever runs for President, he'll probably win because of news pictures from tonight, face to face with his rescued son, all thanks to me kidnapping him.

Next thing I know, the kid's in the other guy's arms. Gabriel says, "Oh Uncle Eugene, thanks for coming." He gives that guy the biggest hug, and his uncle squeezes him real tight and pats him again and again on the back of his head, then puts him down on the street.

Gabriel runs for me now, and I'm full of the willies. I don't know what to think. The little snipe comes up the stairs and wraps his arms all around me. I try to stand off, but he holds me tight. He's looking up at my face, and when I look down at his face, I see he's full of tears. He whispers, "Can't I visit some time?"

"Oh hell," I says. The crazy kid's got something in his mind and he's gonna do it no matter what, so I just put my hand around his head and whisper down to him, "Sure. Sure, but just keep it a secret. Now wipe your eyes."

"Okay. I'm going back to my mom and dad. Bye."

As he goes down the stairs, his mother comes toward him. "Come on, Gabriel," she says. "Where are your shoes?"

"They got burned up in Mister Wagner's fire," he says.

His mother looks up the stairs. "Mister Wagner?" Her face goes white as she searches over the crowd. "Who's he?"

"He—he got me out of the fire," Gabriel says.

Suddenly her eyes flash as she sees me. I'm fidgeting a hundred miles an hour, and my hands don't seem big enough to hide my face behind.

"I see," she says, covering her mouth with her fingertips. "Ahm—why don't you go back with Dad and Uncle Eugene. I'll be over in a jiffy..." Gabriel looks up at her confused, but then takes off for his old man.

I feel like I'm in a corner as she makes her way up the stairs toward me. My hands are closed, sweaty, and I stuff them in my coat pockets. She keeps coming closer, until she's right in front of me. I look at her feet.

"Well, Duncan Wagner!" she says. "I never expected this to be the way we'd meet again."

I look out over the street at the fire engines and the crowds of people milling about. "Small world, ain't it, April?"

"It sure is." She puts a hand on my arm, and I dart my eyes down to look at it. "Hey, thanks for saving my boy."

"Well—it wasn't anything. You know. I mean…"

For a long time neither says a word. I'm getting more fidgety, and my cuts are pinching all over. She lets her hand fall from my arm, and I can feel her looking at me, though I don't dare look straight into her face.

"It has been a long time, hasn't it, Duncan?"

"Yeah. Eleven years and ten months."

She sharpens like she just got slapped in the face. I look straight at her now and feel tears fighting to get to my eyes, but I blink them back. She's looking at me and nodding her head up and down. Her lip is quivering. "I don't know what to say, Duncan. I'm really at a loss. But I want you to know that I really appreciate what you did tonight. The police told us—"

"Sure. It was nothing, really. How've you been, anyhow?"

"Oh, I'm doing okay. I'm happy. We're very happy to have Gabriel back."

"Yeah…" I want to ask her, "Do you ever think about me? You ever wonder what it would be like if you stayed?" But the words get lost in quicksand somewhere between my head and my mouth. I just look at her face and see she's still bright, still as lovely as ever, though in my heart I know she's not as happy as we both would be together, if there was ever a way to turn back the clock and do it differently. But I have to stop burning up over her. I have to find my own way to be happy. I says, "Well, good to see you."

"Good to see you too, Duncan." She starts to turn away, but then she comes back. "You know—I still think about you now and then—the good old days. You used to cook me things on the grill while I made salads with Nellie in the kitchen. And all those times we went to movies and had these intense discussions over pizza? We had such fun times. Well. I better go—goodbye, Duncan."

\* \* \*

The crowd grows, and the photos and the fire go on just about till I can't take it any longer. The cops ask me to go to the hospital, they ask me if I need a hotel, and all I keep saying is I want to find a room at the YMCA or down to the Salvation Army. The heavy cop with the red face tells me he'll drive me to the YMCA if I want, and I says that might be nice.

On our way to the cruiser, I stop to watch Winthrop Booker's road barge go away from the fire engines and the cameras and reporters. Suddenly I feel dead lonesome. I turn to see my apartment getting eaten up by fire. Looking around on the street, I see I don't know a single soul. Already I miss the kid. I know he'll never find me once I get a new place, something I can get with the money he made me put in the bank. Good thing he wasn't chained up that day. Then I think never mind, good thing he wasn't chained up tonight. My brain chokes on the thought of it. I swallow, then turn to the cop and ask him the time.

"Four o'clock in the morning, champ. Come on, let's get you over to the YMCA."

As we get near the cruiser I says, "Tell me, what was all that about a kidnappin'?"

"You kidding?" The cop looks at me and stands still for a second. "That was Gabriel Booker, a State Rep's son. It's been all over the nation all week, where've you been?"

I shrug my shoulders and let him talk some more.

"They almost caught the perpetrator, too, but things got screwed up. From what I know," he says, "they had the ransom stashed in some bushes, and they had a video camera on the bushes all day. So it's almost dark when somebody comes by, some street bum. Plus it's snowing pretty heavy, so they can't get his picture. They get four different plainclothes guys to follow him, and they lose him!"

"Really?" I says. "Four guys?" I think about Dick Murphy, and how stupid I was to put him in that trap without thinking it all out before. It's the first time I realize I could've had him killed out there, and I feel awful shame. It was only a miracle he didn't get traced. I just hope they never put that part of the kidnapping on the news, because if old Murph ever finds out, I'll die before he gets the chance to kill me.

"They couldn't grab him, no way—they had to make sure he got the cash so they could get the kid back safely. But they had orders not to lose him, and they lost him."

"You think they'll find him?"

"Oh, they'll catch up. Get this. They sewed an FM signaling device in one of the money bags so they could keep a trace on it. Only the thing didn't send signals in some areas, they figured it was crossed by radio stations or interference. For a while they thought they picked up somethin' around South Station. They went down there and all they found was two big guys beat up on the street, and no more radio signals."

"Is that so?" I ask. "That something new, that radio thing?"

"Ever hear of LoJack?"

"Oh," I says, all of a sudden feeling lucky.

"The kicker is, I have a niece studying over at Wentworth, and she's been working on this tracking technology. They're using it in cell phones, cars, even on dogs and cats. She's doing a project on getting RFID codes on currency and credit cards, so money can be tracked anywhere."

"RFID?—What's that?"

"That's radio frequency ID. Pretty soon they'll be putting it in kids. Whatever, it's no use on this case now."

He opens the back door of his cruiser and I get in. It's warm inside and smells new. Pretty soon we drive off, and I don't feel much like talking anymore. I'm too wound up with thinking and with lonesomeness, and with knowing I just lost my really best friend in as long as I can remember. Maybe there will be other friends, like Dick Murphy, who could be longer lasting. But that Gabriel was a one in a million kid.

While we ride, I feel myself half awake and half asleep. I put my hand in my back pocket to adjust my wallet, and I think about my ATM card and the bank account. Again I think how lucky I am to have this money. It'll hold me a couple of weeks while I get a real job.

A flash comes in my mind of the art girl, Martina. I don't know whatever made me think of her—probably the wallet, because I stashed her number in there. I just picture her standing there in front of me, showing me that sketch of myself. Maybe I will give her a call some time after Christmas like I said I would. She seems very friendly and like somebody a man could be happy with. I don't think I used to be a real man, anyhow, but now I feel strong and together again. Like being with Gabriel gave me the chance to play father, and through it all my own self got to grow up some. As it goes, I'd have to say that's the best Christmas present I ever got so far, and I expect there'll be better still to come. What do I want, better than that?

# AFTER ALL

How I got caught I would've never figured, because for a while I thought I was home free. Looks like the cops didn't like being showed up after all their work booby trapping the ransom money bag. So here I am in court-ordered counseling, and on probation for three years.

The investigation began right where I sent the cops, to those three guys that mugged me on Christmas Eve. The day after Christmas, this guy named George Grimes got arrested in his apartment in Boston with a hundred thousand in cash. The radio thing they sewed in worked after all. He got charged with kidnapping Gabriel, assault and battery, extortion, possession of narcotics and contributing to the delinquency of a minor, which they threw in because of the cocaine they found on him.

Then, later the same day, the two guys I slammed got arrested in their hospital beds. They got charged with the same crimes, except for contributing to delinquency. There was an easy connection between them and George Grimes, because they happened to complete my original story about the three guys with the boy and the shopping bag, and about how I beat them up in the street.

But all three guys kept insisting they were innocent, and didn't know squat about a kidnapping. They were all grilled separately from the start, and each one of their stories matched up to confirm that their only crime was mugging some guy dressed up like Santa Claus.

So then they go to Gabriel with photos of the three muggers mixed in with a whole bunch of suspects, ask him to point out anybody he recognizes. He can't do it, and tells the investigators that the kidnappers kept him blindfolded. Also, Winthrop and April Booker couldn't identify any of the mugger's voices. They said the voice on the phone sounded different, when it wasn't disguised. And sure enough, the state police did put a tap on their phone lines, but by then I was using that voice toy, so the best they could do was trace the calls to the places I made them.

The cops tried to work their way around the kid's blind-fold story, but Gabriel's parents and counselor pushed the cops not to browbeat him. Everybody thought Gabriel was afraid to identify the real criminals in case they might come back later to get him.

One sharp cop kept working on his own hunches, an investigator named Dave Plaztok. Right from the first ransom call, he said the kidnapping was personal, not political—'cause the ransom was too low for political. He said a hundred thousand bucks was the bargain of the decade. "Booker's got a hundred thousand bucks sitting in the rain on his drive-way, and you're gonna ransom a kid's life?" He said it had to be somebody with a low sense of value about himself, with more interest in the kid than the money, so he looked to Winthrop Booker to see if maybe there might be a mistress in his past, or some former employee who had a grudge. That idea went nowhere, so then he looked to April. She said in the past five or six years, she couldn't think of a single person who might have something against her except maybe the contractor who built the addition, and who they refused to pay the last payment of four thousand bucks because the new stairs cracked and sank two inches, and he never came back to fix it.

After the kid got returned home, this cop came up with another new idea. He figured the story the muggers told was true, that all three of them jumped Santa Claus, and there was no kid anywhere around. They told where and how Santa Claus got cut. Then he knew I fought the three muggers, and had cuts in the same places the muggers cut Santa Claus. So this cop decided I must be the missing Santa Claus, though he knew evidence would be hard to get after a fire. That didn't stop him, of course. He sent a crew to search what was left of my apartment for the Santa outfit, but they could barely get in because the floor, the walls and everything inside was gutted.

Plaztok kept saying that I was the only person ever actually seen with Gabriel Booker. He sent some cops to me, and they asked me all kinds of questions about the three muggers. The trial was supposed to start soon, so there was all kinds of clutter on the news and in the papers about the three suspects and their lawyers. These cops made it seem like the muggers were taking all the blame for the kidnapping. But they kept questioning me, making me feel like some kinda hero until they started getting nosy.

"We searched your apartment and found some cloth from your Santa Claus suit," one said.

"What are you talkin' about? What Santa suit?"

"The lab found some of your blood on the material. Where did you get the bag full of money that had your fingerprints all over it? And do you realize there's a lot of people wondering who started that fire, and if maybe the fire was meant to—say, kill the evidence?"

I got mad, because I never started the fire in my own house, at least not on purpose, and I sure wasn't trying to kill Gabriel or anybody else. I kinda thought they were lying about all the evidence. How would they know the blood was mine, if they never took a sample from me to match? But I couldn't be so sure about the other evidence. They had me cornered, so I had to admit being the kidnapper. They sure didn't get any help from the kid, though. And I was so anonymous, they said, so much to myself, that there were no leads to follow.

It was only after I admitted the kidnapping that April realized the connection to me. She kept saying, "I should've known. I should've figured it sooner." If you ask me, I think she knew it as soon as she saw me on them stairs Christmas Eve. I think it was just too close, too painful for her to realize how much she meant to me.

But that ain't all of it. Now that I'm bagged for kidnapping Gabriel, what do they charge me with?—Panhandling. I get a sentence of three years on probation, plus one year of weekly counseling that I have to pay for myself. They said I could've got life in prison for the kidnapping if the Bookers pressed the case, but I held the wild card—what if I wanted to have tests done to see if Gabriel was my own son?

They told me if a paternity case was opened, it would ruin the Booker reputation and would cause a lot of damage to the kid. I said I didn't really want to wreck the kid's home, wasn't there any better way? They dropped the kidnapping charges. Actually, it was April and their lawyer who pushed for that—they said it could be argued that picking up a juvenile hitchhiker and taking care of him for a week wasn't technically kidnapping. How the kid must've choked to admit about skipping school and hitchhiking, because all his stuff about blindfolds evaporated. But at least he got it out in the open with his parents.

Their lawyer told me that in exchange for them dropping the kidnapping charges, they wanted me to sign an agreement that I wouldn't have any more contact with the Booker family, and that I could never make a legal claim to be Gabriel's father. That hit me a lot harder than I thought it would. I told him I needed to think about it. For the next two days I was in torture, thinking, wondering—I even said some prayers. I want the kid to have a happy life, and I know that means he should stay in his lifelong home. I will never know for sure if he is my own son. I can't tell by looking at him because he looks so much like April. Much as it kills me to know I'll never hear his tickled laughter again, or watch him as he grows up, I realize it's the right thing for him, no matter how I feel. I had to sign it for the kid.

The investigation made them put me through mental tests. They reported that I had normal intelligence, like they couldn't see for themselves, but that I had a deep depression that clouded my sense of wrongdoing, as they put it.

Now that I'm almost done with the court stuff, I'm glad my therapist asked me to keep making these tapes and also encouraged me to keep in touch with Martina. Back on Christmas night, I called her because I was seriously bored being in the YMCA all day. She said she was glad I called, and we made plans to go out for dinner the next day. She's kind of a vegetarian, which don't bother me so much since I already had practice with one. We also went out two more times before I got bagged—once down to Harvard Square to a coffee house, which I never knew they had music shows like that before, and another time to a nice club for a drink. She was kinda mad when I told her the truth about the kidnapping, and how the cops were investigating me. I was sure she'd take a powder, but she didn't.

Martina and I get along like we always knew each other, and she's real pretty and smiles easy and makes me smile, and I can tell she likes me. She took me over to her place in Jamaica Plain and showed me her art work. She got all flustered and girly when she was showing the sketch of me as Santa Claus right over her bed. That's when I took her hand and pulled her in my arms, and gave her the kind of kiss that makes the whole world stand still.

Then one Saturday in the beginning of spring, she showed up at my door with something wrapped in a wad of tissue paper. She gave me a huge kiss and said, "Hurry up and open it." So I opened it and saw my grandmother's Saint Joseph statue, still held together by glue and scuffed with a little fire damage. I guess the cops did look over the apartment after all, and they saved a few boxes of things they would use for evidence if they had to. Martina asked them if they could give up the statue now that the case was cleared, and how could a cop ever look at her face and say no?

I did find myself a legit job, and now I manage an apartment building near Davis Square in Somerville, which gives me a break on rent. It's about the most happening place around Boston, far as I'm concerned. Could be a good place to do my Santa Claus thing next Christmas, if there's time and a real charity that will have me. And now that Filene's is closed for good, and the Enchanted Village of Saint Nicholas in mothballs, downtown Boston ain't what it used to be, anyway. I have a new car—it ain't a Jag, but at least it's better than that old rattletrap Dart with the four bald retreads.

Martina's birthday is coming up in fall, and I'm saving up some dollars to get her a ring and ask her to marry me. And this time if she tries to leave me, I'm gonna camp out on her doorstep, or maybe dress up in a suit of armor and ride a white stallion down her street, and kidnap her for my very own. But no, I don't think I'll really need to do that. 'Cause this time I just got a feeling there's a good chance for the both of us.

## THE END